A PEACOCK SPEAKS

BY

DON PEACOCK

Production and design by Four Cats Publishing

Cover photograph by Donald Jerry, used by permission
Cover design by Tonya Foreman

ISBN-10: 0988839903
ISBN-13: 978-0988839908

TABLE OF CONTENTS

ACKNOWLEDGMENTS

The author wishes to thank the people who helped him get into writing short stories, improving them, and getting them published. These include Nancy Pinard, who taught the short story writing class the University of Dayton's Osher Lifelong Learning Institute, the Wannabes Writing Group for their encouragement, and the Miami Valley Writers' Group whose critiquing has improved my writing greatly.

Finally, a few other people to thank include my wife, Rose, who put up with my spending time on the computer with my writing and wound up being a published author herself. Also thanks to Julie Mitchell, Assistant Dean, Special Programs and Continuing Education at the University of Dayton, and to Denise Quillen, also with the University of Dayton, who manages the daily interaction with students, liaisons, and moderators within the Lifelong Learning Institute. In particular, thanks to Don Hart and his Four Cats Publishing Company for his help in getting this book published.

FREDERIKA

Relaxing on his enclosed patio, reading a book or just watching television was the way Howard Smith loved to finish up his day. Particularly after the day he had had today. The business end of running his restaurant sometimes drained him completely. Overseeing the cooking always buoyed him, when he could spend time on it, but more and more the business end was becoming his biggest job. It hadn't been this way when he started with a small restaurant that served almost all healthy meals. But now that he had turned thirty-five he fully understood that he had to have a couple of hamburgers on the menu. He probably could not have survived for ten years if he had not bent a little bit. There always seemed to be one member of a family group who wanted only a hamburger or a cheeseburger. That was the way a restaurant business went if you wanted to survive.

Howard had just started to relax when suddenly he saw something out of the corner of his eye. "What was that?" he thought. Something had appeared and immediately disappeared. He wondered if he should go check or just stay relaxed and enjoy his evening. Suddenly, there it was again. Something was bobbing up in his patio window. He gingerly rose out of his chair and inched over towards the window.

As he approached the window, he looked down towards the bed of dahlias just outside. Then he saw movement again. It wasn't a rabbit or a bird. It was the biggest cat he had ever seen. He slowly slid the window open in order to yell at the cat. Then he noticed the cat was on a leash.

"What the devil? Cats are never on a leash. What's going on here? Is the leash caught on something?"

Then he saw her. A little girl, looking to be about four or five, crouching behind the largest dahlia bush. He slid the window all the way open to get a better look. The little girl looked up at him, stood up and started towards the front of the house. She was holding the cat's leash tightly in one hand, but the cat trotted right along with her, even leading a little bit.

He called out, "Young lady, what are you doing in my flower bed?"

"I'm sorry," she said as she picked up speed.

He ran for the front door to try to catch up with her. It was almost dark and he wondered where she had come from, or more importantly, where she was going. He knew he had never seen her around the neighborhood before.

As he popped out the front door, he saw her walking rapidly down the sidewalk. He easily caught up with her. As he moved along beside her, he started to ask her questions.

"Who are you, young lady? What is your name? Where do you live? Where are you going? Where are your parents? Talk to me, young lady. Answer my questions."

Finally, with an exasperated tone of voice, she said, "I don't know!"

Finally she headed over to the curb and sat down, still holding the cat's leash very tightly.

"My mother said I shouldn't talk to strangers."

"That's fine under normal circumstances, but right now things apparently aren't normal. So tell me where your mother is and I'll see that you get home to her."

"You can't do that. She's gone and I can't find her."

"Gone where?"

"They took her away."

"Who did?"

"The men with all the flashing lights and the loud siren."

"That sounds like an ambulance. What color was it?"

"It was red and white."

"Yes, that must have been an ambulance. Did the people who took her away say anything?"

"Yes. He said, 'I think she's a goner.' What does that mean?"

"Oh my God," he thought to himself. His next thought was, "This child may be homeless."

"What is your name?" he asked her.

"Ginette. Mommy said it is spelled with a 'G'."

"With a 'G'. That is an unusual spelling."

"Mom said it was for her favorite drink."

"Gin. O.K., that's sort of strange."

"I'm not strange! I'm four and a half years old. Almost a big girl."

"I'm sorry. I didn't mean that you were strange. When was the last time you had anything to eat or drink?"

"This morning. Mommy bought me a sandwich and some milk."

"That was a long time ago. Has your cat eaten lately?"

"No. She's really hungry."

"What's her name?"

"It's Frederika. She's a good cat."

"I can see that. I'll tell you what I'm going to do. Let's go back to my house. I will fix some food for you and your cat. You can eat while I try to see what I can find out about your Mom. By the way, Ginette, my name is Howard. Howard Smith. Come on, let's go back to my place."

"Okay. Frederika is really hungry. I think I am too."

They got up from the curb and headed back to Howard's house. As they entered the house Ginette asked, "Does your mommy live here with you?"

"No," Howard replied. "She lives in Las Vegas. I was out to see her a couple of months ago."

"She would be surprised to see me, wouldn't she?"

"Yes, she would. Are you planning on staying here?"

"I don't know. I miss my mommy. Maybe she could stay here too. Could she?"

"Well, we have to find her first. Now let's get some food fixed for you two. I'll open a can of tuna for Frederika. That should satisfy her for now. For you, I think I will do a hamburger. How does that sound?"

"Great. Can I have cheese on the hamburger?"

"Certainly. You have to have cheese on a hamburger for it to taste right."

Howard got a can of tuna down from the cupboard and started to open it. As the odor wafted out Frederika decided she liked him and walked over and started to rub against his leg. The further he opened the can, the harder the rubbing. Finally Howard put the tuna in a cereal bowl and placed it on the floor as Frederika pushed his hand aside and dove in, eating like she hadn't been fed in days. Then Howard got all the makings for cheeseburgers out of the fridge. Then he asked, "Ginette, what do you like on your hamburgers besides cheese?"

"I like ketchup and lettuce, please. Are they ready yet?"

Howard caught the meaning of her question and started to quickly make patties and get them on the portable grill. The buns and the condiments were set out on the counter ready to make a finished product. As quickly as the burgers were done, they were slapped on buns. The cheese, ketchup and lettuce were added and plates carried to the table, followed closely by Ginette. Howard poured a glass of milk as she started on the burger. He got himself a beer, which he was sure he was going to need before the evening was over. As the munching of the cat, the girl, and the man picked up in volume, Howard was thinking about how best to continue from there.

He picked up his cell phone and dialed the local hospital. When the receptionist picked up the phone he asked if a woman had been brought in that evening from the southwest part of town. The receptionist said yes, there had been one and then asked whether he was related to her.

"No," he responded, "I think her daughter is with me at this point. Can you let me talk to her?"

"I really shouldn't give you any information on her now, but she is in a coma. Traumatic head injury. We don't know how it happened yet. We have been told that it probably was from a fall. You should call the police about the daughter. They will find a temporary foster home for her. How old is she?"

Howard glanced over at Ginette sitting at the table still eating. "No, I think she is probably better off with me right now. Besides, they probably wouldn't let her keep her cat with her. I'll call back tomorrow to see how the mother is doing."

"Sir, I think it is best if you call the police and let them know what is going on."

"My name is Howard Smith. I own the Chateau France Restaurant. I can be reached there during the day. I think Ginette has had enough trauma for today. I'll bring her down to the hospital in the morning to check on her mother. I can be reached at the following number here at home: 454-9903. Good night."

As he turned off his phone he saw that Ginette had finished her sandwich and Frederika was licking her bowl clean. He then said, "Ginette, come to the living room. We have to talk."

When they were settled in the living room, with

Frederika bedding down on the end of the sofa, Howard tried to get more information from the now sleepy girl. He also told her that her Mother was very sick and they might not be able to see her for a few days.

"Did you have any clothes near here? How about pajamas. Anything?"

"Mom left all that in the room we stayed in."

"Where was this room?"

"I don't know. Mommy said we would only be there one or two nights."

"That must be a motel or hotel."

"Do you remember the name of the place?"

"It was something like Sleepy Hollow, I think."

Howard got the phone book and started searching. He finally found a motel named Sleep Better. On a hunch he got on the phone again and dialed the number. He asked the desk clerk about a woman and a little girl who had stayed there last night and whether they had left anything in the room. The clerk said, "Yeah, they left a bunch of stuff. The cleanup people put it all in the trash. It's all gone."

"Oh, crap," Howard thought. "Now what?"

He hung up the phone and turned back to Ginette who was occupying herself with her cat and a piece of string she had found.

"Okay, Ginette, we have to get you some clothes first thing and then we have to get stuff for Frederika. She'll need food and a litter pan and toys to play with, although that piece of string seems to be working wonders."

He quickly dug out a large pan, went outside, and filled it with some soft dirt. He made a mental note to never take that pan to his restaurant. "Well, we have a temporary potty for Frederika just in case she needs one while we go get you some clothes."

He took Ginette's hand and they headed into the garage and hopped into the car. After putting her seat belt on, he started the car. As he backed out to the street he commented, "There's a little shopping mall about five blocks from here. They should have everything we need right now. We can plan on what you'll need from that point. I seem to remember there is a pet store there, also. We'll make a stop there and get everything that will make Frederika happy."

As they drove towards the shopping center Howard asked Ginette about where Frederika got her name. Ginette said, "My mother saw the name in a magazine. I liked it, so we started calling her that."

"How old is Frederika now? Do you know?"

"Of course I know. She's my cat. She's 2 years old. I think. I'm pretty sure. That's what mommy said the other day."

"Where did you get her from? Did you find her?"

"We got her for my birthday. I think Frederika likes for us to do what she wants."

"Oh, here we are. Now to find a parking space close to an entrance. We might have a lot of stuff to carry out to the car," Howard said, as he drove towards the main entrance. Luckily, they found one fairly close, and as he pulled into it he commented, "It always pays to phone ahead and reserve a parking space."

Ginette gave him a funny look and replied, "I don't remember you calling for one."

"It's just a saying for when you get lucky," Howard responded.

After parking, they hopped out of the car and entered the mall, looking for the department store and the pet store. As usual, it turned out that they were at opposite ends of the mall. Then Howard spotted a children's clothing store and headed for it. As they entered a woman approached them asking if they needed any help. Howard said that they did and proceeded to explain that they needed clothes for the young lady, everything necessary both inner and outer. The clerk asked if he knew the sizes and upon his answer of 'no idea' she made a guess and led them over to a rack of small dresses. As they searched through the clothes Howard explained to the clerk that Ginette had lost most of her clothes because they were accidentally thrown in the trash.

After hearing the explanation the clerk picked out three dresses of three different sizes and said they would try them on.

The clerk took Ginette's hand, carrying the three dresses in her other hand, and headed for the dressing room. About ten minutes later they came out with Ginette looking delightful in a pink dress with white trim. As they approached Howard, he got the biggest smile on his face since he had perfected his Shrimp Creole recipe.

"She looks like a very lovely young lady. You picked out the right dress for her."

"Now that we know her size, how many outfits are you looking for and how much in the way of underclothes, shoes and socks?" asked the clerk. "I should tell you that her underwear is in atrocious shape. She really needs all new things."

Howard quickly responded, "That was on the list to get, but I didn't know how to check for sure. I really appreciate you taking care of that. On the whole, I think she needs at least four dresses. Also, at least six sets of underclothes, at least eight pairs of socks and three pairs of shoes, plus two sets of pajamas. What do you think?"

The clerk replied, "Don't get carried away. Remember, at her age she'll outgrow them in six months. I'd love to make the big sale, but I have to be honest with you."

At that point a small voice piped up, "Hey, remember me? I'm still here. I'd like to have lots of new clothes. I never had new clothes before."

"We'll take that under advisement," Howard said as he tried to keep from laughing.

"What does that mean?" came back from Ginette, as she stood there with her hands on her hips.

"I'll tell you later. Let's start looking at clothes."

The clerk led them over to Ginette's size clothes and started to pull some off the rack. As she and Howard looked and discussed the picks, Ginette made sure she got her comments in as well. Finally they settled on three dresses and three pants sets. Then they picked out six sets of underwear, eight pairs of socks, two pairs of shoes, and finally the two pairs of pajamas. As they carried everything over to the cash register,

Ginette danced around them exclaiming about how much she liked her new clothes.

When the total was rung up and announced Howard gulped and exclaimed, "These things are almost as expensive as my clothes are." The clerk broke into a grin, saying, "What did you expect? They're girl's clothes."

Howard pulled out his credit card, finished the transaction and got all the clothes in bags. Then as he tried to get everything collected so he could carry them out to the car he turned to the clerk and asked, "I'd like to get your name so I can make sure I get you when I have to come back for more stuff."

"Certainly. My name is Kathryn Russell. I am usually here in the store every weekday from ten to six."

"Thanks. Next time we need clothes I'll call and make sure you're here."

"I'll be here. I own the store. If you're nice, I might even get you a discount," she said as she started to laugh.

"I'll hold you to that," was his answer while he was thinking, "She is really nice and pretty to boot."

After they put the clothes in the car, they headed back into the mall to the pet store. There they started laying out the stuff that Frederika would need. This included a litter pan, litter to go in it, a food bowl, and a couple of bags of cat food. Then they picked out several cat toys to entertain and play with her. They also picked up a padded bed for her although she usually slept in bed with Ginette. Finally they had everything they would need, paid for it, and took it all out to the car.

From the mall they headed back to Howard's place. Ginette's head was starting to nod indicating she was starting to really wear down. He needed to get her back home and let her catch up on her sleep after a long, tiring day.

On the drive back, Howard tried to gently pry information from her on her background, where she came from, and if she had ever met any relatives that she could remember. Between her young age and her sleepiness, there was very little information obtained. It was more of a race to see which happened first, their arrival back at Howard's or her falling solidly asleep on the seat of the car. In the end sleep won out as the little girl slept the last few blocks, but Howard had gotten one piece of information. Ginette's mom's name was Roberta Johnson.

As they approached the apartment parking lot, Howard saw two police cars sitting in front of the place.

"I wonder what this is all about," thought Howard. As he pulled into a parking place the two police officers approached his car.

"Excuse me, sir, we are trying to find Howard Smith. Would you know him or where he might be found?"

"I'm Howard Smith. What's the problem?"

"The problem is you have a little girl whose mother was badly injured in an accident earlier today. We need to take her down to the station house. You don't have authority to retain her."

"Retain her! What is she, a safety deposit box? She's a little girl who has had a crushing day and is finally sound asleep here in my car. We just got back from getting her some clothes, which she badly needed. I think the best thing for her right now is to stay sound asleep and to try to recover from a terrible day. Her cat, Frederika, probably could use a little sleep also."

"Well, sir, we aren't worried about a cat. It will probably be taken to the Humane Society until we resolve what happens to the girl."

"That would be a terrible tragedy. That cat is the only thing left of importance to her. Her name, by the way, is Ginette. The cat's name is Frederika. The best thing for the two of them, at this point, is to sleep. My guest bedroom is perfect for them. I think we can talk about this further in the morning."

"Sorry, sir, but we can't leave her with you. You don't have the authority to keep her at your place."

"I can probably fix that very quickly. I am a friend of your chief, Tom Warren, as well as Judge Johnson. Let's get Ginette into my place and settled down, then we will make a couple of phone calls and resolve any problems over this."

"Neither one will be in their office at this point. We may not be able to contact them until tomorrow morning."

"I have a way. I have been to both of their homes many times. I can call them at home, explain what happened and I don't think there will be a problem getting this resolved."

With that he pulled out his cell phone, flipped to his list of contacts, scrolled down to the one he wanted and punched the call button. The officer could hear the ringing of the phone and the click as someone picked up on the other end. Then a voice faintly saying, "Warren residence. Who is calling, please?"

"Tom, this is Howard Smith. How are you tonight?"

"I'm fine, Howard. What's going on?"

"I have a problem that I hope you can solve." Then Howard proceeded to tell him the whole story up to and including the request of the two officers, who were standing there listening. Finally Chief Warren asked to talk to one of the policemen. He then got the officer's version of everything before trying to make a decision. Finally, he decided to talk to Ginette who had now woken up. She told him that the only friend she had, outside of Frederika, was Howard. She was crying and asking to stay with him, forever and ever.

After hearing all sides, he told the police officers that they should leave Ginette with Howard for tonight. He then told them he would vouch for Howard as he had known him for about ten years and had always found him to be honest and trustworthy. Also, he said, that he felt that Ginette had gone through enough tragedy for one day. Beyond that Howard had been a long time contributor to kids' charities, donating both time and money without question.

At that point the two officers headed back to the police station and Howard and Ginette headed into the house with all of Ginette's new clothes. As they entered the house Frederika came running to see them and Ginette finally started to grin and be a little happier.

Howard knew that everything had not been settled yet and that tomorrow would be a new ball game. For now, he only wanted to get Ginette and Frederika settled down for the night. It was not going to be very easy after everything that had occurred during the day.

It took an hour but everyone was finally settled down in their beds and ready to go to sleep, Ginette and Frederika in her bed and Howard finishing a glass of wine before jumping into his bed and trying to get to sleep. He knew that tomorrow he was going to have a very full day resolving a lot of problems. He was fully determined to see that he got full responsibility for Ginette, believing that was the best thing for her. Much better than being dumped into the foster child program as well as losing her beloved cat in the process. He also knew that, being single and working up to twelve hours a day in the restaurant, it was not going to be easy.

It took him a couple of hours to get calmed down enough to go to sleep. When the alarm went off in the morning he felt like he had only had about an hour of sleep, particularly when he heard Ginette and Frederika already romping in the living room with the new cat toys. He crawled out of bed and went in to check on the two, finding them thoroughly enjoying the playing and ready to get on with the day.

The first thing Howard had to do was to set up something realistic to take care of Ginette while he was at work. His idea was to have his mother fly in from Las Vegas. She could stay with Ginette during the day for a couple of months. She was retired and a widow since his father had passed away five years before. The possible problem with this plan was his mother might not want to upset all of the new hobbies she had gotten involved with in the last five years. These included knitting, weaving, family genealogy, reading, and writing fictional short stories. He realized he had to convince her that she could still do all of this from his house and computer as well as from her own. At this thought he smiled broadly and decided he would call her around 9:30 that morning to talk about all of this. She couldn't possibly refuse her only son this one favor after all of the free meals he had fixed for her in his restaurant. Except when he found that she had developed an allergy to peanuts. That one got kind of messy with doctor's visits and all that. But she said she had forgiven him. Hopefully that was really true.

Howard managed to wait until close to 9:30 to make his call. When she answered he quickly got into the full story of Ginette and his great need for her help in handling the situation. He made sure to point out the great repercussions for Ginette without the assistance of his kind, gentle, brilliant mother. He was being as persuasive as he could and it seemed to be working.

It turned out his mother had no objection to coming in and helping with Ginette. The biggest factor in this decision was that she felt Ginette needed some stability and sanity in her life at this time. She was actually eager to fly in and meet this little girl that had so captured her son's heart. Prior to this, his whole life had been wrapped up in the restaurant. Now he was finally showing his human side and at the same time trying to do something really good for a young child.

In the end, Mom said that she would try to get a flight the next day. She would let Howard know when her plane was expected to arrive. Howard could pick her up at the airport and, of course, he was to bring Ginette so they could meet.

Howard called his restaurant and told them he had an emergency and was taking the next morning off. He added that he should be in around noon, but he probably would then take the afternoon off. He said that he would explain everything tomorrow.

For the rest of the day Howard spent time trying to keep Ginette relaxed and happy. They spent the time playing various games, like hide-and-seek, or catch-me-if-you-can. Of course Frederika was fully involved in all of them and usually better at them. Ginette fully enjoyed the day, particularly when Frederika was the first one to find her or catch her. At bedtime Ginette had no problem falling asleep.

The following morning Howard and Ginette both awoke expectantly, waiting for the phone call. Ginette was greatly excited and was already talking about 'Gamma' and asking when she would arrive. Suddenly the phone rang and Howard had to race Ginette to get it. It was his mother and she told them that she had a 9 am flight and would arrive at 2:10 pm, thanks to losing a couple of hours on time zones. Howard said he would meet her in the waiting area and that he wasn't sure Ginette could contain herself, she was that excited. Howard's mother had to admit she also was pretty excited about meeting this young lady.

Howard and Ginette had a relaxed morning, getting cleaned up, dressed, having breakfast, and getting ready to go to the airport to meet the 2:10 arrival time. Howard knew he would take the 'girls' to dinner at his restaurant. For now he could just kick back and spend time with Ginette and Frederika and have a light lunch before going to the airport. He was looking forward to an enjoyable dinner, talking to the two of them, and not having to work. He expected there would be many questions from the staff, particularly about Ginette, and he knew he would have to tell them all about the child, but he figured he could put that off for a day or two. The general picture would do for now.

The forty-five minute drive to the airport approached hysterically funny at times, usually followed by an extremely serious moment as the two of them, but mostly Howard, started to realize big changes were occurring. Both of them became very quiet as Howard turned down the airport access road and started to look for a parking space. After finally getting parked they headed into the terminal and then paused to watch a big jet coming in for a landing. Howard looked at his watch, saw it was a couple of minutes after two and commented to Ginette, "That's probably Mom's plane landing now. We better pick up the pace so that we're there when she comes out of the gate area. We'll need time to get through the airport security."

The two of them got through the checkpoint more quickly than they expected since they had nothing to show and they were not carrying anything. Once through they started to walk faster while looking for the waiting area for Gate 15. The plane had not made the gate yet but they could see it taxiing in.

The two of them sat down in the waiting area where they could keep an eye on the plane as it approached the gate. After what seemed like an eternity, the walkway was pulled up to the plane, the airplane doors opened and people started coming into the waiting area. Howard caught sight of his mother as she entered the waiting area. He grabbed Ginette's hand and headed over to where she stood looking around. She spotted him and moved quickly towards them. As they hugged in greeting, Ginette stood tugging on Howard's pants leg until he bent over and picked her up.

Turning to his mother, he said, "Mom, this is Ginette, one of the nicest young ladies you will ever meet." Then to Ginette, "Little kid, this is my mother, Martha Smith. I know you two are going to really like each other." Martha gave Ginette a big hug and they headed out to the parking lot and the drive home.

As Howard drove back to his place, the three of them talked a mile a minute about each other, the situation, the future, and how to keep control of all of it. Primarily the talk was about Ginette, her future, and about Ginette's mother in the hospital still in a coma. Ginette couldn't follow everything they said but she knew most of it was about her.

After a brief stop at Howard's place, they all piled back into the car and headed for his restaurant. All of them were a little quieter on this part of the jaunt knowing they could work on the problems later. For now they wanted to relax and enjoy a great dinner.

As they approached the restaurant Howard was pointing things out to Ginette about the downtown area. Ginette mostly pretended to be interested, while anticipating the restaurant and dinner.

Howard pulled into a parking space beside the restaurant and they hopped out and headed in. The hostess, a young, good looking girl, just inside the door saw Howard and said, "It's about time you got to work. It's a good thing this place can run itself."

Howard responded, "Be careful, Janet, you can get assigned to taking out the garbage, you know."

Janet replied in a joking manner, "You wouldn't do that. You know all of these customers only come here to see me." She then said, "Mrs. Smith. It's good to see you again. When did you get into town?"

Martha said, "I flew in this afternoon."

Janet finally saw Ginette standing close behind Howard. "Who is this young lady? I don't think she's been here before."

Martha replied, "She's the one who brought me to town. Howard will have to tell you all about what's going on."

As Janet was taking them to a table she was pointing Ginette out to every employee they passed. Several of them followed the group to the table and stood there waiting to hear the story.

"We're hungry. At least let us get our orders in and then I'll explain the whole thing." The wait staff went back to work but kept an eye on Howard's table, ready to cluster around it again. They didn't want to miss a thing.

Finally, with orders in and twelve people standing around the table, Howard started to give them the short version of what was going on. He went through finding Ginette, catching up with her, taking her home, and finally, at the insistent urging of Ginette, he told them all about Frederika. He then explained that his mother had flown in to help take care of Ginette. He tried to parry as many of the questions as possible and was finally rescued as their dinners arrived at the table.

As they ate, the talk turned to the things that needed to be done. Martha brought up the idea of getting Ginette into a preschool since there were two very good ones within five miles of where Howard lived. They finally decided it was a good idea and that they needed to explore it more. Throughout this Ginette kept asking if Frederika could go to preschool with her. She obviously did not want to be separated from her cat for a long time. She didn't understand completely that Frederika, at this point, was her only connection to her mother, but the feeling of it was there.

Howard and Martha tried to make dinner as pleasant and comfortable for Ginette as they could while still discussing what needed to be done. They decided Howard would check on the preschools within the coming week. Then the future possibility of adoption was brought up by Martha, something that Howard had not considered at all before now. Howard realized it would depend on what happened with Ginette's mother.

As they finished their food and prepared to leave, several of the wait staff came back to the table with more questions about Ginette, suggestions on how to handle things, offers of babysitters, and general well wishes. Howard jokingly told their waitress to send him the bill. As everybody started to laugh, she responded, "That's OK. We know where you live." Howard put a good tip on the table and the three of them headed for the door. Just before going out, he told Janet that he would be in on time in the morning and would be in for the day. The young lady said, "Darn. That'll mess up the day," and started to laugh. Howard pointed at her as he walked out the door grinning.

On the drive back to Howard's place, they were all fairly quiet with most of the noise being Ginette continually asking if they were going back to see Frederika now.

Back at the apartment, Martha went to Ginette's room to go over the things that Howard had bought such as the clothing, any toys, and stuff for Frederika, etc. When she finished she came out and told Howard, "You only bought dressy outfits. She will need some rough and tumble clothes like shorts, jeans and tops. Where did you get the clothes?" she asked.

"It was a children's clothing store in the mall. The owner helped me pick out colors and fit, but at the time I didn't think of shorts and jeans."

"OK. Tomorrow evening we'll all go back and add some stuff to the wardrobe."

They all settled down in front of the TV for the evening with Howard and Martha catching up on family things and Ginette romping with Frederika with the piece of string she had found the day before.

The next day Howard went to work leaving the three girls (Martha, Ginette, and Frederika) to fend for themselves until he got back home. He told them he would be back about 5:30, they would get supper and then they would go get the rest of the clothes for Ginette. Before he left he had the 'pleasure' of cleaning Frederika's litter box because his mother said she certainly wasn't going to do it.

All day at work Howard was pestered by the staff with questions about Ginette: what might happen to her and what could they do to help. They all really liked her and were willing to do anything they could to help Howard. Howard answered most of their questions he could at this time. Questions about Ginette's mom were parried but only because the only answer he could give at this point was that she was still in a coma, getting no better or no worse.

At about 1 pm a man walked in the front door of the restaurant. Howard knew immediately he was a police detective, just by his manner. He asked Janet where Howard was and she pointed him out. He walked over to Howard and said, "Mr. Smith, we have to talk. In private."

Howard expected the worst and he got it. Ginette's mom had passed away mid-morning. With no known relatives, the hospital had the body transported to a local funeral home for now. The detective said they needed to talk about burial of the body and the disposition of the little girl. Howard quickly responded that the only 'disposition' of the little girl that was allowed would be to leave her in the care of himself and his mother. The detective said he had no problem with that. He thought it was the best thing all around for her at this time.

Howard told him he would help with the funeral arrangements if he would be allowed to do so. The detective said he was sure there would be no problem with that. He then gave Howard the name and telephone number of the funeral home and asked him to go ahead and contact them to make the arrangements.

After the detective left, Howard called home and told his mother what had happened and what he planned to do. He requested she keep everything on hold until he got home and between them they would tell Ginette. As he headed home Howard had trouble keeping his mind on driving while thinking of the right way to tell Ginette about her mother. He was not looking forward to this but it had to be done. This also reinforced the possibility of adoption that he was now considering. He fully understood that being a single male made it all the tougher to adopt a young girl. He knew he would need the complete help of his mother, Police Chief Warren, and Judge Johnson. He also felt that his standing in the community would help ease the way.

On the drive home, his mind was all over the place considering possibilities, planning, and preparing himself for what he had to do. In the final consideration he decided to just be as straightforward as possible, but, at the same time, be as gentle as possible. As he approached his place he had made up his mind as to how he would handle telling Ginette about her mother. He first had to discuss it with his own mother and enlist her aid. Entering the house, he called to his mother to find out where she was. She answered, "Back here. We're in the family room. Come on back."

Entering the room Howard saw Ginette laid out on the floor playing with a toy car with Frederika chasing the car as Ginette moved it around on the rug. Seeing her playing with Frederika made his job harder. Delivering really bad news is tough enough, but to do so to a young girl who has had such a difficult time lately was just about going to break his heart. Seeing the apprehensive look on his mother's face didn't help him at all. He asked his mother to join him in the kitchen. Once there he told her what he had to do and how he was going to do it. He also told her that he was paying for a small funeral and buying a grave site for the burial. She concurred so they went back to the family room to talk to Ginette.

"Ginette," he said, "come sit with me. We need to talk about your mother."

"Is she coming home?" Ginette asked.

Howard's response was to tell her that her mother had already gone home. That she was in Heaven looking down on them and would be watching over Ginette to make sure she stayed safe and happy. He told her he and his mother would be there for her always. He skipped over the part about there being a number of hurdles to clear in the near future.

Ginette finally understood what she was being told and started to cry while moving over to Frederika and picking her up. She clutched her cat very tightly, continuing to cry.

Howard and his mother went over to her and while they had a group hug, Howard told Ginette that they loved her and wanted her to stay with them always.

After a few minutes Howard said, "Just remember she is in Heaven and watching over you the same as she had done before the accident."

With that Martha gently took Ginette's hand and led her back to her room to try to get her to go to bed and, hopefully, sleep. In about fifteen minutes Martha returned and sat down with Howard to discuss what they needed to do in the next day or two.

"I think she will be okay. Frederika is still with her and I'll look in on her in about fifteen minutes," Martha said. "I'll go with you at that time," Howard said. "I need to see that she is all right. It's amazing how quickly you can get attached to a little darling like that. I will take on anybody who tries to take her away from us."

The next morning Howard started to make the necessary phone calls. The first was to the funeral home to discuss arrangements, then to Chief Warren and to Judge Johnson to see what he had to do to start adoption procedures. Both of them said they would fully support Howard in the adoption process and they saw no obstacles to accomplishing it.

After a late breakfast that allowed Ginette to sleep as long as she wanted, Howard, Martha, and Ginette went to the funeral home to make final arrangements and to let Ginette start saying final goodbyes to her mother. Later in the afternoon, as a needed change, they took Ginette back to the children's clothing store to get the rest of the things she needed.

As they entered the store, the owner, Kathryn Russell, smiled broadly and jokingly called out, "I knew you couldn't pass up the quality of the clothes that I carry in my store." She came over to greet them and was introduced to Howard's mother. At that point Howard indicated for his mother to take Ginette around the store to look for what they needed while he proceeded to tell Kathryn the story of what all had happened. Kathryn tried to offer some words of consolation but she understood none could be sufficient. She asked if Ginette knew about it and when she was told yes, a tear appeared in her eye, which she quickly wiped away and tried to put on a happier face as she went over to talk to Martha and Ginette. As Ginette wandered through the clothes looking, Kathryn and Martha discussed the whole thing. Martha told her Howard was going to start adoption proceedings, but they would be more complicated than ordinary because Howard was not married. Kathryn's thought was she was glad to hear that since she did find him attractive. She then said to Martha, "Maybe I can help that situation." She went over to Howard and offered to help take care of Ginette, if Howard was interested. She told him that, because of his work situation, she could have Ginette in the store during the daytime a couple of days a week with no problem. She added that they could even make arrangements for Frederika to be there since almost all of her customers enjoyed seeing animals, particularly a friendly cat.

The first thought that Howard had was that he could really get to like this lady. He then said, "Thanks. I'm sure my mother would like to have some time for her own things once in a while." Then his second thought was that he may have found the woman for him. Aloud he asked, "Would you like to have dinner sometime with all of us? It would only be a group of four."

Kathryn responded she would be delighted to have dinner with them anytime, and to just let her know when.

Howard found he was finally having really good feelings about the whole situation and was, more than ever, sure that everything would turn out all right. He was already looking forward to seeing Kathryn again.

On the way home he told his mother about inviting Kathryn to dinner. Her only response was, "I think that was a really good thing to do. How about this weekend? You have been working too hard and you need to get a life. Maybe Ginette and Kathryn are going to be it."

THE WEDDING

"Could I ask you something?" John said. "Do you mind if I don't go to the wedding with you?"

"But you're the groom. You have to be there. What are you thinking?"

"Well I told you I would rather elope than go through all of this. I still think it's foolish to spend all of that money when we could use it for other things. We could just slip across the Nevada state line, go to Vegas, and have a nice wedding there."

"But all of the invitations have been sent out. What do we do about those? It would make us look ridiculous."

"Maybe, maybe not. Think what we could do with all of that money. I can think of a hundred things. I was talking to Mary, your maid of honor, about it yesterday. She had all kinds of things to suggest. She's a very smart girl. She is also very pretty. I found her very interesting to talk to."

"What are you talking about? You just met her three days ago."

"I know, but we talked like we had known each other for years. She is very easy to talk to. Why don't we call this whole thing off and make other plans?"

"When you say 'Call the whole thing off' what exactly do you mean?"

"I don't know. I think I need to talk to Mary about it."

MY OTHER GRANDPA

It was an old church, established one hundred and fifty years ago. Yet the pastor, Charles Pogue, was fairly new to his job, having been hired from a southern church only two years before. He brought great credentials with him in both preaching and leading a congregation. He also excelled in working with children. He put in many painstaking hours making sure he did his job right. He had established several groups of games combining young children and their parents or grandparents. Two that everybody thoroughly enjoyed involved a youngster, either a boy or a girl, age five to seven, and their grandfather called Question and Answer-Move on and Race Style Scavenger Hunt. This evening they were going to play the Question and Answer game. The fathers that had not yet achieved grandfather status could hardly wait until they could join in the fun. Non-qualified adults enjoyed sitting along the sides of the room and just watching. It was rapidly becoming one of the most popular things in the church and there was talk of expanding it to two or more afternoons per week.

On this particular evening the room was almost completely filled with nineteen child and grandparent teams eager to get started. The seats around the walls were completely filled with people talking about everything in the world, but in particular who might win the game today. Yet standing alone in one corner of the room was a young girl. She was about the age of six, and she eagerly, even nervously, looked around the room and watched the entrance to the room. Something was obviously bothering her. Finally Pastor Pogue, noticing this, walked over to talk to her.

"Mary, you look like something is wrong. Can I help you?" he asked.

"I don't know, Pastor. My grandpa was supposed to be here by now. We've been looking forward to this all week. I don't know what's happened to him. Mom dropped me off and had to go on to work. She wasn't going to pick me up for a couple of hours since Grandpa was supposed to be here."

"Let me see what I can find out," replied the Pastor.

The Pastor went to his office and called the grandfather's number. A man answered and asked, "Hello. Who is this?"

"This is Pastor Charles Pogue from the Third Baptist Church. I'm trying to locate Mr. John Parker. Is he there?"

The voice responded, "I am from General Hospital emergency medical team. Mr. Parker has fallen and injured his back. We were just leaving to take him to the hospital. It doesn't appear to be a serious injury, but he is in pain, so we have sedated him. Do you have a phone number for one of his close relatives?"

"No, I'm afraid I don't. Mr. Parker's granddaughter is here at the church right now. Her mother is supposed to pick her up here later. All I can offer now is that I will give her the information when she gets here."

"Okay. I guess we have to settle for that right now." The EMT then gave Pastor Pogue the phone number to call at the hospital.

Pastor Pogue headed back to the game room to see what he could do with the situation. When he entered the room, little Mary was still standing in the corner and it appeared she had been crying. He went over to talk to her and tell her that her grandpa was not going to make it to the church. He didn't want to make things worse by telling her that he had been injured. After he told her she did start to cry quietly.

"I really wanted to play in this game," Mary commented. "I really like this game where you answer a question and if you are right you move forward on the life size game board."

"I am not sure right now what we can do. Let me check around with the crowd here," was the Pastor's reply. He stepped to the middle of the room and got everyone's attention.

"Listen up. We have a young lady here who needs some help. Her grandpa can't make it here this afternoon. Is there somebody here who could help out by taking his place in tonight's game?"

At that point an elderly gentleman raised his hand and said, "I hadn't planned on anything like this because I'm new to the church here and I was just trying to see what all went on, but under the circumstances I think I will change my mind. I am willing to help out in any way I can."

"Mr. Johnson, we appreciate your offer. If you will join me I will introduce you to your partner and we can get started with this evening's game," said Pastor Pogue with a big grin on his face.

He and Mr. Johnson went over to where Mary was standing and Pastor Pogue introduced them. "Mr. Johnson, this is Mary. Be careful she is really good at this game. Mary, this is Bill Johnson and he is going to be your partner today. Bill, the rules of the game are that you have to answer a question and if you are right, you get to move forward one space. You have to draw the question out of a box and there are ten bonus questions that allow you to move forward anywhere up to ten spaces. Good luck."

Mary looked up at Mr. Johnson and said, "Thank you for helping me. What should I call you?"

"Why don't you just call me 'Grandpa Bill' for tonight. That is probably the easiest thing," was the response she got.

The twenty contestant pairs walked out on the floor, drew numbers for starting position, and then the game began. The first four pairs missed their first question. The next five pairs managed to advance one square. Mary then stepped forward and drew a question out of the box. The people around the room started to applaud. She had drawn the bonus card awarding ten spaces for a correct answer. The question involved physics. It was, 'Who was the most famous German-American physicist?' It turned out that Bill Johnson had a PhD in physics from MIT, so that was like asking somebody what 2+2 equaled.

"Einstein, Albert Einstein," Bill yelled out. He then eagerly took Mary's hand and started to advance ten spaces before the guy running the games could say 'Correct'.

The rest of the afternoon proceeded on that path. Mary drew eight of the ten bonus cards and Bill yelled out eight correct answers. At the end they had reached the finish line before the second place pair was a quarter of the way there. 'Grandpa Bill' and Mary had laughed, high-fived each other, and thoroughly enjoyed the whole thing. They particularly enjoyed the standing ovation that the whole room gave them. Mary was just beaming with enjoyment. The other nineteen pairs could only stand and applaud. The first place prize was four tickets for free meals that a local restaurant had donated.

While they were celebrating Mary's mother entered the room and came quickly over to her. "Where's your grandpa?" was the first thing she asked.

"I don't know," Mary replied. She continued, "We won, Mom. We won."

At that point Pastor Pogue came forward and spoke up. "I need to talk to you about that. Let's step over here for a minute."

They went over to the side of the room, leaving Mary and Bill to celebrate with the snacks that had been provided. The Pastor quickly got into the conversation he had had with the emergency medical workers, emphasizing the comment that it appeared nothing was seriously wrong with her father. He continued, telling her that they didn't know where she was at that point and they did not have her cell phone number.

Mary's mother pulled out her cell phone, gave the number to the Pastor, and then dialed the number for the hospital that the Pastor provided to her. When the receptionist answered she asked about her father. After providing the information that she was the man's daughter the receptionist checked and told her that there were only bruises and he was ready to go home whenever someone could be there to pick him up. Mary's mother said she could pick him up on the way home and that she could be there in about twenty minutes. The receptionist said they would have him ready and waiting.

Don Peacock

Mary's mother then went back into the game room, over to Mary, and asked, "What do you mean 'We' won? Who is this 'We'?"

At that point Bill Johnson stepped forward, introduced himself and began to explain what had gone on. The Pastor joined them and helped with the explanation. He also formally introduced them with, "Sarah, this is Bill Johnson, a new member here at the church. Bill, this is Sarah Williams, Mary's mother." At that point Sarah turned to Bill and thanked him profusely for what he had done to help her daughter.

"I hope you don't mind, I asked Mary to call me 'Grandpa Bill' during the game," Bill said.

"No problem. I think it worked out great. When her real grandpa is feeling better we have to have you over to the house to get more acquainted."

"That would be nice. You have a really great daughter there. She is really sweet as well as being a beautiful young lady. By the way, Mary and I won four coupons for free meals in the game today. I would suggest splitting them up. One each for you, Mary and your father. I will keep the fourth one."

At that point Mary and her mother headed out to pick up the grandfather at the hospital. On the way Mary got a full explanation of what had happened to her grandfather, emphasizing that there were no major injuries.

Bill headed home to get things ready for his son's visit the coming weekend. When Bill got home he checked his email and found a message from his son saying what time he expected to arrive the next day. Bill noted it was late enough in the day that they should plan on eating at the new restaurant that had

36

just opened up less than a mile from where he lived and it was the same one that had provided the meal coupons for the church game. With that he decided that he better sweep the guest bedroom and straighten things up. With both his and his son's wives no longer alive, cleaning was something he didn't worry about nearly as much as he should. With that thought, he got busy with the sweeper and dusting cloth and spent an hour doing a passable job.

The next day Bill's son rolled in at four thirty in the afternoon. They had a lot to talk about. Bill on what had happened at the church, his son about his promotion in the robotics research company he worked for. They also had many other things to go over because it had been six months since they had talked face to face.

Bill very quickly raised the point of supper and said that he had a coupon for a free dinner at the Golden Nugget and they could then split the cost of the second dinner. Don thought this was a very good idea. It would give them the chance to continue talking while they ate and relaxed over a drink or two. They headed out to Bill's car and on to the restaurant.

At the restaurant the hostess said that all they had right then was a table for five but they could be seated there. After being seated they ordered iced tea to drink while they looked over the menu. There was a continuous stream of people coming in to eat. About ten minutes later the front door of the restaurant opened and in walked Sarah, Mary and Grandpa Parker. The hostess told them there would be a short wait for a table for three. As they waited, Mary looked around the place and suddenly called out, "There's Grandpa Bill!"

Sarah looked over and said, "So it is. Let's go see

him before we get seated." They were almost all the way to the table when Bill looked up and saw them. He got a surprised look on his face, and then a great big smile. He rose from his chair and gave Mary and then Sarah hugs.

He looked at Grandpa Parker and proceeded to introduce himself, telling him that he was the one who had been his granddaughter's partner in yesterday's game. Bill finally got around to introducing his son, Don, to everybody, telling them that Don was in town for the weekend.

At that point the hostess came over and said that they had a table for three ready. Bill interrupted, saying, "Why don't you three join us here at this table? There's plenty of room."

Everybody liked that idea and seated themselves. Mary quickly grabbed the chair between her real grandpa and her play grandpa so she could talk to both of them. Sarah sat down by Don, after he jumped up and pulled the chair out for her.

Sarah commented, "Thank you. Gentlemanly acts seem to be on the wane lately. I appreciate it. Thank you again."

With all of them seated, they got their orders in, and the conversation around the table got rolling with Mary talking to both grandpas at the same time and Sarah and Don having a long discussion about themselves, their work, their hobbies, and anything else that popped into their heads.

As they finished eating, Sarah commented that she had to find someone to help her move some furniture tomorrow. She had gotten a new sofa and easy chair and had to completely rearrange the living room. She also mentioned that her father had planned on helping, but she wouldn't let him now because of his back injury.

Don then said, "I can give you a hand with that. It shouldn't take very long."

"No, I can't let you do that. You are here to visit with your dad. That should come first."

"I'll have the next two days with him, so how about if we move the furniture tonight and get it out of the way."

Bill got into the discussion saying, "Sarah, why don't you drive Don to your place and take care of the furniture. I'll follow in an hour or so and bring Mary and your father back to your place."

Don stood up and said, "Let's go now and take care of it. Okay?"

Sarah agreed and she and Don left. Bill, Mary and Mr. Parker stayed to talk and take care of the tiny bill. The two grandpas decided to relax over a beer while Mary had an ice cream sundae.

On the way back to her place, Sarah and Don continued the discussions they had started at supper with each one eventually telling how they had lost their spouses. Sarah's husband had lung cancer combined with a bad case of pneumonia and had passed away four years ago when Mary was only two. Sarah explained that Mary had almost no memory of her father. That was why she enjoyed doing so many things with her grandpa. The games at the church are a good example. Don then proceeded to tell how his wife had been killed in a car wreck when a drunken driver ran a red light. It had happened four and a half years ago.

They had just starting to talk about having children.

Finally they reached Sarah's house, parked, and went in to attack the furniture. It took only about an hour to run through three different setups of the furniture to see which might be best. At that point Don was pretending to be all out of breath and completely worn out while Sarah was having a continuous laughing fit at his antics.

Just then Bill, Mary and Mr. Parker walked in and started to laugh at the whole scene that Don and Sarah were putting on.

Sarah asked if everyone would like a piece of cherry pie and some coffee. There were three quick 'yes' answers while Mary asked if she could have a cookie and some milk. Sarah said that she had set coffee before going out to eat and had turned it on when she and Don got back to her place, so pie and coffee would be ready in about two minutes. She headed out to the kitchen and Don followed her saying, "I'm pretty good at cutting pie, so I'll give you a hand."

Everyone else took a seat on the new furniture and then listened to all of the laughing coming out of the kitchen.

Finally pie and coffee came out of the kitchen into the living room, and everyone was warned that they better not spill anything on the new sofa and chair. After eating, Bill said that they should be getting home and letting the three of them relax for the rest of the evening. As they headed for the door, Don asked Sarah if she had an email address. Sarah said yes and wrote it down while Don was writing his down for her. Then Don and Bill went out to the car and drove home with very little talking. Bill asked Don if he had enjoyed the evening and Don could only say, "Immensely, immensely."

The following week it started with an email every week, and then it increased to one every few days. Finally it reached one a day plus a more detailed letter each week.

After six months of emails and letters and four visits by Don, Don sent an email, "If I emailed you and asked you to marry me would you accept?"

The response he got from Sarah was, "If I emailed you and asked you to marry me what would you answer?"

Within an hour the answer came back from Don, "I'll go first. Will you marry me?"

He received an email ten minutes later. "Of course I will, you idiot."

"I know that I'm an idiot, but you aren't allowed to call me that more than once a month."

"How about if I alternate it with 'honey'?"

"That's okay. I will just call you wonderful, lovely, beautiful, intelligent until I can think of something better."

"How about 'wife'?"

"Bingo. I think you got it."

"Now we have to tell everybody."

"I have a feeling that they already know," responded Don.

"When can you come back here so we can tell everyone?" Sarah asked.

"I'll take off work the next two days and be back there tomorrow by noon."

"That sounds great. I'll fix supper here and we can tell everybody and start to make plans."

The Saturday seemed like a long time coming for both Sarah and Don, but at last they were all collected at Sarah's place, seated around the table and just finishing supper when Don rapped on the table to get everyone's attention.

"Listen up, people. Sarah and I have an announcement to make."

Bill turned to Parker and said, "I think they should give each of us one guess and I think we all would get it right."

"Don't get sarcastic, Dad. Just listen up. Sarah and I are going to get married and we want Pastor Pogue to perform the ceremony."

Bill turned to Parker again and said, "Oh gosh. I would have never guessed that."

"I told you not to get sarcastic. Wait till you get the bills for the wedding."

At that point Bill looked over at Mary saying, "It looks like you might really be able to call me 'Grandpa Bill' in the near future and between your real grandpa and me you are going to win a lot of those games at the church."

THREE TERN STORIES

CHECKERS ANYONE?

John had really looked forward to his visit with his younger brother Harry. This would be John's first time in the town where his brother now lived. He had planned for a while to visit him and had finally managed to work things out for a week's stay. They had not seen each other for five years. During the week he was there his brother was giving him the grand tour. They had visited the courthouse, the new library, the downtown square, the new sewage plant, and two of the three parks in town. As they left the second of the two parks, Harry asked him if he wanted to see the giant checkerboard that the city had built and where people took the place of the checkers.

"Yes, I really would enjoy seeing that," said John.

"It is in this next park, the third one we had planned to visit," Harry answered. "It's right on the shore of the lake."

He explained that the squares were two and a half feet on the sides and the people actually stood on them and then moved positions as the two players told them where to step. It was fun and extremely popular on a nice weekend day.

He further explained that the only problem they'd had with the game was the number of terns that liked to rest on the board after feeding in the lake. The lake attracted them to the area because it was well stocked with small fish. The townspeople had spent a lot of time in the park with the birds and actually found that they could train them to stay on the black squares. They did this by leaving them alone when they landed on a black square, but when they were on a red square one of the townspeople would pop them with a very low power BB gun that would just scare them without hurting them. The terns quickly learned to just stay on the black squares. This way the people didn't have to clean the bird droppings off the squares as often since they only used the red squares for their checker games.

After a short drive John and Harry arrived at the park and walked over to the giant checkerboard. John quickly noted that all the terns were staying only on the black squares. He asked Harry how, really, had they accomplished this. Harry replied that they had just enforced the one basic rule: No tern on red.

SAVING THE BABY

John and Cindy Thompson were enjoying a leisurely walk around Lake Boko. They enjoyed walking there because the scenery was so nice and the ocean beachfront was only two hundred yards away so they could see the waves breaking on the beach while they strolled around the lake. Another thing they enjoyed at this lake was that they also got to see a variety of animals, both ocean shore and lake front types.

As they walked, they heard noises up ahead of them. Curious, they picked up the pace to see what was happening. As they stepped around a stand of bushes they saw a baby robin on the edge of the lake. It was raising quite a fuss. Apparently it was just beginning to fly and had left the nest and struggled through the air for the short distance to the lake's edge.

Then the couple spotted a large grey house cat that

was creeping up on the baby robin. The parent robins were in the closest tree adding a great deal of noise to the melee.

At that point John and Cindy saw a tern flying over from the beachfront to see what all the noise was about. It then proceeded to add a lot more noise while circling over the cat. Then suddenly, the tern dive-bombed the cat causing it to duck down, pivot, and run toward the covering bushes. As the tern climbed back up into the air, making as much noise as he could, the cat recovered and started back towards the baby robin.

The whole process started again. The yelling, the diving, the ducking, the running, and the climbing back up.

After watching the whole process being repeated, John commented, "That tern must have had good intentions because it was saving the life of the baby robin."

Cindy replied, "Yes. I agree with you."

The whole process was repeated for a third time. As the fourth round commenced, a second tern came flying in from the beach front and dove down, startling the cat, and causing him to decide his prey had too much protection so he promptly vacated the area. As the cat disappeared into the woods the robin parents flew in and, with their encouragement, got the baby to struggle back up under the tree where he would be safe.

Finally the two terns flew down and landed on the edge of the lake. They started circling, apparently looking for food or fighting. As they slowly circled each other John commented, "Those two terns have done a good job of driving that cat away and protecting the baby robin."

"Yes," said Cindy. "They did a very good job. It was nice of them."

Then they noticed that the terns were dancing around each other, not looking for food.

"I think that's a mating dance," said Cindy.

"I think you are right," John replied. "Which works out well, because one good tern deserves another."

THE SICK BIRDS

It was only a small beach at a hidden lake. Many years before some local people had trucked in sand to form the forty-foot long beach on the water's edge. They obviously enjoyed the serenity of the lake area. There were very few people who were aware of this lake beach. Many small animals came down to the lake to drink. Also, all kinds of birds could be seen on all sides of the lake. These included doves, robins, sparrows, a hawk now and then and the ever-present terns, which were usually to be found at any small body of water in this part of the state.

The only people ever seen here were residents who lived within five miles of the lake and had found what a pleasant, secluded spot it was, a tremendous place to relax and get some sun without being bothered by anything. Also, obviously, on occasion a few casual nude sunbathers would spend a day here knowing the odds that they would be disturbed were almost zero. Occasionally a nude couple would be there doing other things than sunbathing, such as splashing in the water, taking pictures of the scenery around the lake, or just watching the animal life come and go.

Then one day a couple who had come to the lake to do some fishing and sunbathing noticed a tern laying by the water's edge. They went over to check it and poke it with a stick to see if it was dead. This didn't disturb them too much as dead birds had been found by the lake's edge before. Their deaths usually appeared to be from one of numerous natural causes. The couple then noticed a second dead tern about twenty feet away and further back from the lake shoreline. They decided this was very strange and that they needed to check around. Eventually they found two more dead terns and felt that something very unusual was going on. The man used his cell phone to call a local veterinarian who was a friend of theirs. They told him what they had found, describing the appearance of the birds in great detail. Finally the veterinarian commented that there had, lately, been several occurrences of terns dying from an unknown virus. The virus was lethal to terns only, and he suggested that, if they could, they should bury the four terns to help prevent the virus from spreading. He assured them that the virus was not harmful to humans even though there was no way to save an infected tern that caught the virus.

The veterinarian also told them they should look around to see if any other terns were showing symptoms of the virus in order to determine if it was spreading. The symptoms they should look for included erratic flight and not calling constantly. Terns were usually very smooth fliers/gliders and made a lot of noise while in flight. The couple started walking around the lake keeping a close eye on the terns they found. Overall, they saw at least a dozen terns that seemed to show the symptoms that the veterinarian told them to look for. They called the veterinarian back and told him what they had seen. He told them that drastic action was probably necessary.

The couple went back home and called all of the neighbors they could locate. They passed on the information they had learned, including what they had seen at the lake, and asked each one what they should do about it. A large majority of the people said immediate action was necessary. Several suggested they needed to take 22 caliber rifles out and start to eliminate the terns that were infected. They felt it was the only solution possible. If they didn't do this now, the virus could very easily be spread to other areas and produce an epidemic.

Five people volunteered to go out to the lake with their guns and try to help solve the problem before it got out of hand. They met on the side road that meandered out through the woods to the lake. They left three cars there, piled into the other two cars and finished the drive to the lake. When they reached the lake they parked about fifty yards away so as not to stir things up too quickly. They decided they should split up, three one way and two the other way going around the lake, and that since all of the terns were very likely to have already been exposed to the virus they should eliminate all of them. All five got their rifles each with five shells in them. They started to spread out and head toward the water. As they separated and started around the lake, they started shooting the affected terns that they spotted. After twenty minutes they had to return to the cars for a break and to reload.

At the cars one of them asked, "Where did you put the box of shells?" Everyone stood there with blank looks on their faces. Nobody answered him. Finally one guy said, "I bet it is in one of the cars left back down the road." A second guy remarked, "I think I remember placing it on a table in the garage. I bet it is still there."

Then they started to debate about whether to go home and leave the job undone. Finally they agreed that they needed to find some other way to finish what they were doing. Just then a third man looked over and saw a pile of rocks, probably left there when the beach was built. An idea popped into his head. "Hey guys, there were only about ten terns left and all of them appeared to be somewhat disabled by the virus. I bet, with these rocks, we could finish them off, bury all of them, and go home to have a few beers."

With that they all grabbed as many rocks as they could hold and headed back to where the terns were. As they started back the guy in the lead called out, "Remember people, leave no tern unstoned."

BREEDING IS EVERYTHING

As Virginia sat at the lunch table waiting for her order of a sandwich and a salad, she started thinking about her life and her dogs. She was single, divorced, not rich but very well off, and loved being involved in the world of dog shows. She was very self-confident but also felt her one real lack in life was that she had never had any children. In reality, her Dobermans were almost certainly a replacement for children. She was only thirty-five and still felt she had the chance to have children. The problem was a husband she was compatible with and could love. That let her first husband completely out of the picture. Compatibility with him meant giving up too many things she really loved. That was why he had had to go. It had been three years now since the divorce.

Just then she saw Harriet Dorald approaching her table. She had known Harriet as a slight acquaintance for a year or so, but never got close with her. Harriet and her husband were also in the hobby of showing Dobermans. Harriet's husband was the most active at the dog shows, although Harriet was well skilled at showing the dogs also. The difference was Harriet was much more defensive of their dogs than her husband. She was always very careful to keep people away from her dogs, particularly her champion male, His Majesty King Bruno. In the same way, Harriet was also very protective of her husband. In reality she was very dependent upon him since he was the one with the very large income. In fact, he was quite wealthy.

As Harriet approached she spoke up very suddenly, "I want you to leave him alone."

"Wha-what are you talking about?" came the reply

51

from Virginia with a totally surprised look on her face.

"You know what I mean," said Harriet. "I saw you earlier over there petting him and making over him, just because he won Best in Show and is the most valuable purebred Doberman in the state. I would like you to know my dog is extremely important to me."

"What are you talking about? I was just admiring him. You know I breed Dobermans, and besides my female Champion Princess Portia Starbright has almost as many Best in Shows as your champion male. I'm just here trying to have a peaceful dinner and recover from the rigors of the show."

"I thought the whole subject needed to be brought up and discussed. This seemed like as good a time as any," said Harriet.

"Well, breeding your stud dog, Majesty, to my bitch Princess seems to me to be a natural thing to do since she is the top female Doberman in the state. The puppies would be extremely valuable. Worth about fifteen hundred dollars apiece for the females and one thousand dollars for the males. I would be willing to pay you a very good stud fee."

"I bet you would," Harriet fired back. "Majesty usually gets a fee of one thousand dollars with no guarantees."

Virginia then almost politely urged Harriet to leave as her meal was just arriving at the table. As Harriet turned to leave, she commented that they would continue this conversation later.

The next day, with both ladies in a more sociable mood, they got together at lunch to further discuss the breeding of their Dobermans.

"You should know my husband has a say in whether this goes ahead. It really is his dog more than mine," said Harriet.

"I've met your husband a couple of times," responded Virginia, as she sheepishly looked away for a second. "It was at shows in Los Angeles and San Diego where we both had dogs entered."

"That is possible. I didn't make it to those shows. I had some family commitments that urgently needed taking care of, but Jonathon said he enjoyed them and things went better than he expected. But he usually does have high expectations. It comes naturally to him. He is almost always a leader in anything he gets involved in. I don't like to brag but my husband's family is quite wealthy. He is not only descended from a long line of European royalty, but he has also achieved great success in his own right." Harriet usually would not admit that she had married into great wealth when she married Jonathon because she suffered somewhat from a lack of self-esteem because of her own more middle class background.

They are quite proud of themselves, thought Virginia. Then she said, "I had to take care of some business last week. I had to consult with some designers about a new line of clothing I am bringing out next year. I call it 'the Portia line' after my Doberman. Then I had to check on the several charity shows that I host." It was well known that Virginia had risen to near the top in the clothing design field. She was well-respected, very self assured, and always got what she wanted.

At this point Harriet tried to change the direction of the conversation by asking, "You said you had met my husband at the California dog shows. What did you think of him?"

"I, I, I can't really say. I didn't get to know him that well. He seemed very nice. I remember he didn't talk much," Virginia spoke in a hushed tone of voice.

Harriet paused a second and then said, "Well, that's not like him. He normally talks constantly."

She then excused herself to go make a phone call saying she had to check on an appointment. She walked over to the corner of the room and punched in a number on her cell phone. As she stood there talking on her cell phone her husband entered the restaurant and immediately spotted Virginia sitting at her table. He swiftly walked over to her, grabbed her hand as she tried to withdraw and said, "That was a great weekend we had in San Diego. I could do that again anytime."

Virginia stood up to leave, mumbling something unintelligible and obviously trying to depart as quickly as possible. Just then Jonathon felt a hand hit his back and heard his wife's voice saying, "Just what does that mean?"

He spun around, aghast. He then started to mumble, "I was talking about the dog show. It was great."

"I don't think that's what you meant. You and that bitch made a connection, and I don't mean her dog."

"No, no dear. We just went to the dog show and came home," Jonathon blurted out.

"No, you didn't. You came home two days after the dog show ended. You had the handler bring Majesty home. You claimed that you were examining a new, elegant bitch for breeding purposes. Just what the Hell were you doing?"

"Please believe me, that is exactly what I was doing."

Harriet felt all her emotions kick in as she fully realized what had happened between Virginia and her husband. She felt hurt, insecure, somewhat dazed, and furious. She poured all of that into her comments.

"Let me guess, it just happened to be a human bitch you were examining. I'm going to talk to my lawyer. When I get done with you, you will be a lot poorer."

Harriet then turned to Virginia and said, "That goes for you, also. Both of you will be hearing from my lawyer in the very near future. And I will own both dogs before they are through."

Virginia turned very pale and ran for the ladies restroom. Jonathon turned very red and started stammering, following Harriet as she left the restaurant headed for her lawyer's office.

And that is the tale of two well-bred males and two elegant bitches.

TEETOTAL OR NOT TEETOTAL

Everybody in the bar looked up as the policeman opened the front door and walked in. All eyes followed him as he walked over to the bar and asked to talk to the manager. They could see the bartender flinch just slightly as the policeman continued to stare at him. The bartender then said, "Let me go get him. He's in his office in the back."

The policeman said, "I'll wait here, or maybe I could go back to his office and talk to him there. Your choice."

After a quick glance around the bar the bartender replied, "Let's go back to his office. It'll be quieter. We're pretty full out here and rather noisy."

"Okay. Lead the way," said the policeman as he glanced around the room. He then followed the bartender past the bar and down a short hallway leading to a door marked, "Manager."

The bartender knocked on the door and called out, "John, this is Bill. Do you have some time to talk?" as he glanced down at the policeman's name tag, "to Officer Patteris?"

The manager quickly opened the door and invited Officer Patteris into the room. As he headed into the room Bill commented, "I need to get back out front. If you need me for anything, just give me a shout."

"Okay," John said, as he ushered Officer Patteris over to a chair next to his desk. "Now, what can I do for you?"

"We have a problem and we need to find a solution."

"Okay. I will do what I can to help, whatever the problem is. Sit down and let's discuss it."

"We have to do something about the drinkers leaving the bars and wandering around in the downtown area. They are becoming a nuisance and the merchants are really starting to complain about it. The drinkers are mostly all inebriated and carrying a drink with them. As long as they are walking there is no specific law against it. We need to find some way to get them to stay in the bars. Plus, we really need to do some checks on designated drivers."

Officer Patteris further commented, "A real part of the problem is that as they wander around town they are always greeting each other by raising their drinks in the air and calling out common drinking phrases such as 'Here's looking at you', 'Down the hatch', 'Bottoms up', 'Here's to you and yours', but the most used comment is 'Skoal'. They all seem to know each other somehow. I think it is because most of them have been doing this for some time."

"I know a lot of them have been coming into my bar for years," said John. "They seem to be sober when they come in but not always when they leave." This gave Patteris one more notch of information.

John thought for a few seconds and then said, "I may have a couple of ideas on this, but I need to work on them. Let me get back to you tomorrow."

"Okay," replied Patteris. "I'll stop by tomorrow afternoon and see if anything has jelled."

Before John went back to what he had been

working on he went out to talk to Bill about a thought that had just occurred to him. He proceeded to tell Bill what he and Officer Patteris had discussed. Then he went into some detail on the idea that had occurred to him. When he finished Bill had a big grin on his face and was nodding his head in approval.

Bill jumped in with, "That's a great idea. It should make those drunks think about what they are doing. At least it might slow them down a little. I know where we can get the signs we will need very inexpensively once we get the go-ahead."

"I'll present all of this to Patteris tomorrow afternoon. I think he'll like it. I also think it will be effective without costing too much and without upsetting anyone too much," John responded.

The next morning, John sat in his office working on a write-up on his suggestion. The phone rang. He picked it up. It was Officer Patteris. They talked for fifteen to twenty minutes and Patteris finally approved John's idea as an important first volley in solving the drunks downtown problem. They further discussed implementation of the plan. John said that his bartender, Bill, could get the signs made very cheaply. They would have enough signs made so that all twelve downtown bars would be covered. The cost per bar would be extremely minimal.

When Bill came to work John told him to take off and start work on getting the twenty-four signs they would need. John said that he would handle the bar for as long as was necessary.

Bill immediately headed over to the sign company to put in the order. The company agreed to finish the job in two days. That meant the signs would be available for the weekend when the wandering drunks were usually at their worst.

While Bill was working the sign part of the job, John was serving drinks and snacks and when he had a chance he would call one of the other eleven bars to talk about what was being planned. All eleven of them loved the approach and were ready to proceed as soon as the signs were available. They were all happy to be involved.

Two days later, everything and everybody were ready to go. The signs were quickly delivered, and workers at all twelve bars got busy posting the signs just outside and just inside the entrances of each bar.

As the evening crowds started to arrive they all noted the new signs on the outside of the bars, which were in places where they couldn't be missed. Once inside almost all noted the signs on the inside of the doors. Everybody was discussing the signs and fully understood why they were there.

At every bar someone always pointed out the signs and why they were probably there. In each place the bartender made a point of stating why the signs were put up.

The sign on the outside, seen as people came in, said, 'ENTERING SKOAL ZONE', while the sign on the inside, seen as people exited, said 'END SKOAL ZONE'.

THERE SHE GOES

He had many thoughts going through his mind as he headed for the mall. Just two days before, his girlfriend of four years had told him to take a long walk off a short pier. She gave him the excuse that he wouldn't commit. She was ready for marriage and a family, while he hadn't given those kinds of things much thought. Finally he was starting to understand that he needed to start making many changes in his life and his attitude towards other people. He had spent his whole life committing as little as possible. That probably also explained why he had never risen above the level of Associate Professor at the Regional University where he was employed. Teaching physics and mathematics was what he wanted to do, but he was often assigned to teach related courses, such as chemistry. He didn't particularly enjoy that, but he had also never voiced an objection. He usually just went along with what was done. In fact his whole life was aligned to the passive. Even the car he was driving could be described as non-descript. It was a grey, two-door 1949 Ford coupe. He had owned it for ten years. He inherited it from his great uncle who had bought it off the showroom as a brand new car.

As he neared the Macy's parking lot, he was in the process of deciding he would start making some changes in his life, such as new dressier clothes, shorter haircut, and maybe grow a beard and mustache. He was even beginning to consider the possibility of some adventurous trips such as a cruise around the Hawaiian Islands or an African safari or a tour of Europe. He still felt he needed to talk to some of his married friends in order to get a better understanding of what he needed to do to accomplish his new goals in life.

He was so completely lost in his thoughts that he really wasn't paying full attention to his driving, which was unusual for him as he usually concentrated on what was going on around him, particularly around the mall because of all of the bad drivers who seemed to populate these malls. He looked out the side window and quickly stepped on the brakes. "What in the blazes?" he blurted out loudly. He had to look for a second and finally a third time before he could believe his eyes. There was a little girl, apparently no more than four, walking through the parking lot like she knew where she was going and was making sure she was going to get there as soon as possible.

He came to a stop at the curb, hopped out, and headed after the little girl. His steps, being three times as long as hers, helped a lot, but she was really hurrying along. He caught up with her just as she started to step out into the street. She seemed totally unaware of the cars that filled two lanes and were filled with people concentrating on where they were going to make their next purchase. Being run down by a car is not a pleasant event, but she was almost certainly too young to understand that.

He reached out and grabbed her under the arms, hoisted her up, and carried her back into the parking lot. "Now what do I do? I can take her back to the mall and start searching through stores for her mother or I could just call the police and turn her over to them." He finally decided on a combination of these. He took her hand and walked over to the bench at the bus stop. After they got seated he started to try to get some information from her.

"What is your name?" he asked.

"Mary," she replied.

"What is your last name?"

"I don't know."

"What is your mother's name?" He continued.

"Betty" was the response he got.

"What street do you live on?"

"I don't know."

"How old are you?"

"Three and a half."

"Are you hungry?"

"No. I want ice cream."

"Where are your parents?" he continued.

"Mommy is in there," as she turned and pointed towards the mall.

"My daddy is gone," she continued.

"He's gone? When is he coming back?"

"Mommy says he's not."

At that point he knew that there was a divorce or a death in the family.

Having collected those bits of information, he decided to go into the nearest store and have the mother paged. If that didn't work he would call the police. Taking little Mary's hand, they started over to the store. He was taking small steps so she could stay with him, even though from earlier experience he knew she could show some real speed when she wanted to do so. She was mostly skipping along beside him saying, "Ice cream. Ice cream, please." He assured her they would get some ice cream somewhere nearby, but first they had to find her mother.

He was aware he was taking a big chance by not just calling the police and letting them handle it. He could be accused of child napping even though he had most certainly saved her life and was just trying to reunite her with her mother. With these thoughts he really started to waver, pulling out his cell phone and getting more serious about calling the police. As they entered the store he started over to ask a saleslady where the main office was, but at that point he saw a very pretty young lady frantically looking down all the aisles, calling, "Mary! Mary!"

Just then Mary called out, "Mommy!" Mom turned quickly, seeing Mary and started to run towards her. She reached Mary, grabbed her up, hugged her and then said, "Don't you ever do that again. I have been frantic looking for you." She then looked at the man standing there and asked, "Where did you find her?"

His first thought was that she was very good looking. He then replied, "She was just about to go into the street over here. I caught her right at the curb. Three more feet and she would have been in trouble. I guessed you would be in this store since it was the closest one, so I brought her back in and was going to have you paged."

"How could you page me? You don't know my name."

"Actually, Mary told me your name was Betty. I would have just paged 'Betty, your daughter Mary is in the store office.' I knew that would be all I had to say."

"You're right. I would have come storming to the

office. I really appreciate what you have done in helping her and maybe saving her life. I know how headstrong she can be sometimes. I am really glad you were around today."

"How did she get away from you?"

"I had her right beside me and was looking at some dresses for her. I turned to ask a saleslady a question and she just disappeared. I didn't think she could do that so fast."

"After seeing her racing across the parking lot, I can believe she could do that. She is going to be a top-notch sprinter when she grows up. By the way, my name is Bill. Bill Bowers."

"My name is Betty Forester. I'm glad that you were here and that you acted as you did."

"Why don't you join me for an iced tea and maybe a sandwich while we discuss how to keep your little speed demon under control?"

With that, Betty laughed out loud and said that would be fine with her. She picked up Mary and they headed across the parking lot to a Frisch's sandwich shop. As they went they tried to point out to Mary all the cars going by and telling her that she could get hurt really badly by going out into the street. Mary pretended to listen while interjecting, "Ice cream," as often as possible.

As they entered the Frisch's shop Mary started her chant again. "Ice cream. Ice cream." Betty was busy trying to tell her that they all had to eat something before they could have dessert. She was trying to point out that they could go to Graeter's ice cream store next door after they had eaten or have something at Frisch's, but it was for dessert.

They were seated in a booth with a booster seat for Mary and started looking over the menu. Bill and Betty opted for cheeseburgers followed by cherry pie. Betty ordered a child's meal for Mary followed by a scoop of ice cream. While waiting for the food to come, they discussed general topics like the weather and some TV shows. Finally Betty started asking Bill some more specific questions.

"How long have you lived here in Cincinnati?"

"Eighteen years. My parents moved here when I was five years old. I really call this my hometown rather than Chicago, where I was born. What about you?"

"I was born and raised here. My parents still live here."

"My father passed away five years ago. It was a heart attack. My mother still lives here. I have Sunday dinner with her every week."

"That's nice. I get together with my parents about every three weeks. They weren't happy with the guy I married and they let me know about it. They are pushing me about wanting to see Mary more often."

"I would think that is a reasonable request. Is she their only grandchild?"

"Yes, I am an only child, so Mary is their only grandchild. Unless of course you count the time the Martian came to town and the sextuplets I had with him."

"Now I know you're pulling my leg. I heard about

the Martian, but I know he only liked green-skinned girls."

Betty laughed and said, "Good comeback. You're right. I never met the Martian when he was in town. He spent all of his time with the Mayor."

They both started to laugh at the same time. Mary suddenly broke in to ask when her ice cream was coming.

"Our food is just now getting here so it won't be long," Betty said.

"Oh, all right!" Mary responded with a tone of 'I can't wait' in her voice.

As they ate, Betty pursued getting more information about Bill. In response to questions about what he does, any girlfriends, any hobbies, what does he do for fun, for relaxation, etc., Bill's answers gave a very accurate description of his life. He was an associate professor in physics at a local university. No girlfriends since two days ago, hobbies included sleeping in front of the TV and having a beer in the evening, which was what he did for fun and relaxation.

Although Betty herself was not the partying type, she was starting to get a very good idea of why his girlfriend had left him. She probably couldn't fall asleep in front of the TV or something like that when she wanted to have a good fun evening.

Then it was Bill's turn to ask the questions. Where did Betty work, did she have hobbies, how did she relax, where was Mary's father, did she want to go to dinner tomorrow night?

Betty's answers were straightforward for the mother of a young girl. "I am an executive secretary for the CEO of a local company. My primary hobby is taking care of Mary. I get to relax after Mary goes to bed."

She paused a bit and as a tear rolled down her cheek, she told about the accidental death of her husband, Mary's father. He was working on a team building the new library when a wall collapsed. He and one other worker were killed. It happened two and a half years ago when Mary was a year old so she never knew her father. She herself wasn't sure, at the time, if she could survive the tragedy, but finally she realized she had to survive it for Mary's sake. That is what pulled her through the entire incident. Finally she asked Bill where he had in mind for dinner and was Mary allowed to come.

"Absolutely, absolutely," responded Bill. "It wouldn't be right without her. Should I bring the leash for you know who?"

Betty started to laugh while Mary gave them both a perturbed look and asked, "What happened to my ice cream?" Just then the waitress came walking up carrying a single scoop hot fudge sundae and Mary's eyes lit up.

"I like ice cream. Did you know that?" Mary asked to nobody in particular.

Bill answered, "Yes. I think we all figured that out. Now start in on that ice cream or I'll sneak a spoon in there and get some for me."

At that Mary pulled the dish in close to her and started eating while Bill and Betty continued talking.

"Now Bill," Betty asked, "where was this fabulous place you are going to take us for dinner tomorrow night?"

Her eyes started to twinkle as she watched his face flush as he tried to think quickly. He paused for several seconds and finally blurted out, "How does Doubleday's sound? They have some very good meals and a lot of smaller sized meals for Mary, as well as," and at that point he lowered his voice and placed his hand over the side of his mouth towards Mary and whispered, "sundaes."

The next evening Bill picked up Betty and Mary and drove to Doubleday's where he had remembered to make a reservation. After they were seated and had placed their orders, Betty and Bill continued their discussion to try to learn more about each other. As they talked they began to understand the good and bad points of each other and to realize they actually had a lot in common. Betty was very pleased that Bill got along with Mary so easily and Mary seemed to like him as well, plus he seemed so intelligent even if he was somewhat nerdy. Bill was happy that Betty was such a good mother, so good looking, and had such a good job.

Finally, when the food was set on the table they both were relieved to sit back and concentrate on their meal. Mary had been quiet up to this point while looking around the room at all the other diners and the waiters and waitresses running back and forth. She was finding it all very fascinating. Betty and Bill were also very fascinated but with each other. As they ate, they both felt that the future was looking much brighter. Bill was also deciding that commitment was something he could start to like.

THE FIVE-BLOCK WALK

This is the story of Gary Stone's evening in June when he was just twelve years old. It was a nice, warm, sunny evening, and on this day Gary decided he would walk the five blocks over to his best friend's house. At the age of twelve he was just old enough to not worry too much. It was also an age that when fear hit it could really blow him away. What really blew him away was the breath of the giant goblin that spotted him walking towards his friend's house. Gary was walking along all alone and not paying much attention to what was going on around him. This is the first clue – you should always pay attention, since you never know what could happen. Doing otherwise can sometimes create all kinds of problems.

The goblin started breathing more heavily as he approached, giving Gary the full extent of his sour, rotten egg breath. Gary's first reaction was to try to hold his breath, but that only lasted twenty-five seconds. By then he had to breathe, foul odor or not.

The goblin got tired of blowing all that air on Gary, and he started down the street looking for more kids, but only those in the age group of nine to thirteen years old. He knew they were most susceptible to his breath and could not ignore the foul smell.

But, back to the story of Gary Stone. As the goblin left, Gary turned and headed on toward his friend's house, which was four more blocks away. He had walked only a half block when a witch jumped out of the bushes and said, "Stop right there! I am Henrietta, the wicked witch of the South. Or was that of the East? I am nine hundred years old and I keep forgetting lots of stuff. Right now I can't remember why I jumped out of the bushes. Can you tell me why?"

"No I can't. I don't understand why anybody would do that, and you never told me why. I was just walking over to my friend's house down the street. Do you usually jump out at people?"

"Well, I usually either scare them or eat them. Whichever is most convenient and depending upon my mood."

"Well, that doesn't seem to be a nice thing to do, " said Gary.

The witch sniffed the air and asked, "What is that terrible odor I smell?"

"I just ran into a goblin in the last block and he blew his foul air on me."

"Well that ensures that I won't eat you. Nothing tastes worse than leftover goblin smell. That means you were supposed to be scared. Why weren't you scared? You are being totally uncooperative. Do you realize that?"

At that point Gary turned to go on his way, saying, "Yes, I know that, but I think you are more funny than scary."

"Well now you have hurt my feelings. I will have to go back to witches school for retraining. That will be the four hundredth time I have had to do that in my nine hundred years of life." With that she spun around three times and disappeared in a large puff of smoke. Gary looked around, somewhat startled, to see if she really had disappeared. Yes, she had, so he proceeded on his way.

As Gary crossed the street and stepped up on the curb, a blast of fire went over his head followed closely by a loud roar. Gary jumped, turned, and nearly went into a state of shock as a dragon came walking towards him. He prepared to run but was stopped short in his tracks by the dragon's glare and another blast of fiery breath out of its mouth.

As the dragon approached closer Gary quaveringly asked, "Wha-wha-what do you want with me? I've never bothered you. Go away, please."

The dragon's response was more flame and smoke followed by a loud deep voice, saying, "I am Bector, the evil dragon and I am going to see if you are plump and tender enough to satisfy my appetite. I haven't eaten in three days and you look like you could be the solution to my problem. Hold still while I check and see."

At that the dragon reached out with one front foot and poked Gary with a two-inch long claw on his big toe. Gary's reaction was to jerk away and start laughing. He commented, "Don't do that. I'm ticklish there."

The dragon got a very angry look on his face and said, "You are not supposed to laugh. I am a dragon, a very fierce, scary beast. You have hurt my feelings. I may even start to cry."

"I'm sorry," Gary said. "I'll try not to do that again if you will promise not to tickle me. Is that a deal?"

"I guess so," said the dragon, as he started to perk up. "If you'll excuse me, I see a couple of kids in the next block that I need to go scare. Maybe they will be more cooperative than you are."

With that the dragon flapped his tiny wings and

tried to fly away, but his tiny wings couldn't hack it with a big dragon body. This put the dragon in a snit as he stomped away muttering under his breath. "I sure miss the old days when people had some respect for us poor dragons."

As Gary crossed the next street he thought to himself, "This has been the most interesting walk I have ever taken." As he stepped up on the curb and started onward he suddenly felt a cold chill. He looked over to his left and saw what looked like a small cloud or mist, which quickly materialized into a figure. No, not a figure eight, it was obviously a man, but a man you could see through.

"Wh-who are you? Are you a ghost? I've never seen a ghost before. Are you going to hurt me?"

"No," the ghost said. "Ghosts can only scare you. We are really good at that usually. Are you scared yet?"

"I think I am. I'm not sure yet. You seem too friendly to scare people."

"That's why I am a ghost. I'm John Forth and I used to be the meekest man in Minneapolis, Minnesota. My punishment for being so meek was to become a ghost and go around learning to scare people. You aren't helping me at all."

"Well, if I get a frightened look on my face will that help at all?"

"I think it's probably too late now," said the ghost. "I think you would need to do that and also run screaming 'mommy'."

Gary replied indignantly, "I'm twelve and I don't run screaming 'mommy' anymore. I'm sorry but I can't help you out. There are a couple of kids two blocks east of here. You might give them a try. Maybe bagging a double will help you out."

"Thanks. I will go give that a try." With that the ghost floated off to find the two little kids, and Gary continued his walk. He thought it was probably a good thing there was only one more block to go and then he could relax and play with his friend. Surely the strange occurrences were over and he could finish his walk in peace.

All at once he heard what sounded like a horse trotting down the street. "How can that be," he thought. "No one in this neighborhood has horses."

He saw coming up on his right the biggest horse he had ever seen, and it was ridden by what looked like a knight in armor. As the horse and rider pounded down the street, the horse humped its back and tossed the knight onto the curb. A little bit bruised but otherwise not hurt, the knight got up, straightened his armor, walked over to the horse, and laboriously hauled himself up into the saddle. He took the reins and prodded the horse to continue on. As they approached Gary, the horse, once again, tossed the knight off into the street. As he started to duplicate his labored remount, he stopped, looked at Gary and said, "I hope you aren't going to laugh. That would really upset me."

Gary was shaking, not because he was scared, but because he was trying so hard to suppress laughter. He finally asked, "Why do you get thrown off the horse that often? Do you need riding lessons?"

"Don't get smart with me, kid. If I get upset you're in real trouble. That horse always catches me by surprise when I'm thinking about something else. I think he can read my mind. The longest I've gone without getting thrown was about one hundred feet, and that was only because I was concentrating as hard as I could on his ears. They always twitch just before I get tossed. Of course, they always twitch when a fly lands on them also, so I can never tell what his intentions are."

The knight continued, "I am called the 'Evil Knight', but I don't have time to be evil. I spend all my time just climbing back into the saddle."

"Well," said Gary, "that may be to the good, if you don't have time to be evil. That makes him a nice horse, doesn't it?"

"Well, that may be true. But that would also make me a good knight by default, wouldn't it?"

"I think that may be true," said Gary. "But more likely that does really make him a nice horse."

"I told you not to get smart with me, kid. If I could move faster in this armor I would come over there and give you what-for."

With that the knight climbed on his horse and headed on his way. Gary watched him get thrown off and climb back on three more times. Then he headed on towards his friend's house, which was the first house in the next block. As his friend came out to meet him, Gary called out, "Hi, Jim. I'll have to tell you about my walk. Maybe your mother could give me a ride home later. I think it would be easier." His friend just looked at him and then prepared to throw him a Frisbee.

I DARE YOU

"Oh, come on, Douglas. I don't believe you. You can't broad jump twelve feet and pole vault fifteen feet. I just don't believe you're that athletic."

Since broad jumping was too easy to prove right or wrong Douglas decided to go in the direction of pole vaulting. "Look, Heather, I'm not prepared to prove it right now. I just ate a big meal and my favorite vaulting pole is at home. It got wet last night in the storm and it will take at least three days to dry sufficiently to be used. Using it sooner could be dangerous. You wouldn't want me to get hurt, would you?"

"Let me think about that for a while," replied Heather. At Douglas' unhappy look, she apologized quickly and said she was just trying to kid him. While she said this she was obviously trying to stifle a laugh.

"I don't think that's funny. That's the kind of thing where someone could really get hurt. I'll keep checking my vaulting pole a couple of times a day and let you know when it's ready."

"I don't think you really know how to pole vault so I won't hold my breath. I can better spend the time going shopping. As a matter of fact, my nephew has a birthday in two days, so I'll be at the mall. You have my cell phone number so you can contact me if you want to admit I'm right. Bye for now." She then hopped into the 1998 Chevrolet her parents had bought her for her sixteenth birthday, started it, and took off. The last thing Douglas saw was a hand waving to him out the driver's side window.

"Well," thought Douglas, "at least it's a five-finger wave. Someday I'll learn not to play with her head."

With that he headed over to the library to see if they had a "Pole Vaulting for Dummies" book. He certainly hoped such a book existed. Without it he wasn't sure what to do since he had never even seen pole vaulting let alone having done it. But he knew he wasn't going to let Heather get ahead of him on anything. Douglas knew he would see her later that evening since they both were in the same church group that got together every Thursday evening. He was sure that the discussion about pole vaulting would be continued somehow.

Upon leaving the library and knowing that there was not a book on pole vaulting, Douglas thought he would check with the local college to see if they had a pole vaulting team, although he had never seen anything about one in the local paper. The phone call verified what he was afraid of hearing. No team, no information. He knew now that he was in deep doo-doo and that his only chance was to bluff it out and hope that she would back down. Act brave, act dominant and win. The thought running through his head was that that had never worked before with Heather, and this would probably not be the first time it did. He could see that this might involve a lot of taunting and teasing and near nasty comments.

It had been like this for at least ten of the fifteen years they had known each other. They had grown up together and enjoyed each other's company but had always been competitive. They enjoyed the back and forth of trying to outdo each other.

Later that evening, as the church group was breaking up, they continued the pole vaulting discussion. Douglas was pushing hard with his comments trying to get Heather to back down or even quit. It wasn't really working, but he knew it was the only chance he had. Finally it reached the point of no return for Douglas as Heather said the words that could not be turned down. "I dare you to prove you can pole vault." Between them the "dare" was the ultimate statement that sealed everything in stone.

"Are you really going to dare me?" asked Douglas.

"You bet I'm going to dare you," was the response.

He grinned as he turned towards her and said, "You know if you dare me I have no choice but to do the pole vault. That would have to be the final result."

At that point Heather finished the game by commenting, "Let's go get an ice cream sundae and think about this."

On that note the matter was closed until the next time because Douglas knew that the next time he would catch her in an exaggeration on something. This was the way it had gone for all the years they had known each other.

MY GRAND CHILDREN?

I am absolutely certain that my grandkids are the most perfect grandkids who ever existed. The middle one, Thomas, who is seven, is at the age, intellectually, of a fourteen year old. He is a straight A student and is now in the sixth grade, four grades ahead of most of the kids his age. There is also talk of his skipping the seventh grade. He may well enter college at the age of twelve. Phenomenal! Also he is extremely polite and respectful of his elders. He can be counted on whenever help is needed on something, anything. He loves to please people.

His athletic ability may be even better than his intellectual abilities. Since the first grade he has been very far ahead of all of his classmates in the three sports he loves. These are tennis, soccer, and lacrosse. His serve in tennis is something to behold. A year ago a professional tennis player, rated number five in the world, came to the school to encourage the kids to play and to stay active, because it would improve their whole life. After he talked to the kids he hit some tennis balls with a few of them. Thomas was the third one he hit with. Thomas aced him twice. He had the pro mumbling to himself about how could this happen with a seven year old.

In soccer, Thomas is the star of the team even though the other kids are three to five years older than he is. He is faster than they are. He can change direction with the ball so fast that a lot of them have taken a tumble trying to keep up. He is the leading scorer for his team and has pulled out over a dozen games basically on his own. Lacrosse is not his favorite game but he is still the leading scorer and has won seven of their games for them this year by scoring against three to four defenders.

Thomas's older sister, Lois, is no slouch either. At the age of nine she is already a sophomore in high school and probably will enter college next year. The teachers don't know what to do with her because she invariably knows more about a subject than they do. She has been known to take almost the whole class period lecturing while the teacher sits back and wonders if she is in the wrong occupation.

Lois has already selected the topic for her PhD thesis and from what little I know of physics, I have no doubt she will change the world with its results.

Lois is always credited with being the prettiest young lady in her school as well as being the top scholar. Everybody who sees her is stopped in their tracks by her beauty. She is already receiving requests from Hollywood producers concerning trying out for their pictures. This is to be expected as she has been the leading lady in the last five school plays and she always receives rave reviews in newspapers as far away as three hundred miles.

She is almost as good in sports as her younger brother, Thomas. She is the leading scorer on the girls' basketball team and has been the direct reason for the team winning their last ten games. Even though she is not the tallest girl on the team, the coach keeps moving her to the position of center. This is due to her jumping ability. She has won first place trophies in the last four track tournaments in both of her specialties, high jump and long jump. She gets more height and distance in these events than even the senior girls do.

Billy, our third and final grandchild, at the age of six, is no slacker in the area of brains or athletics. He has just started school, going directly into the third grade, thus bypassing grades one and two after flying through the exams to test his knowledge of the subjects. He has a strong interest in becoming a medical doctor and specializing in cancer research. He has already read everything he could find on it and can discuss the current state of such research in great detail with some of the best people in the field. He goes to the library twice a week looking for any new books concerning cancer research, and he is on the AMA mailing list concerning any new developments in this specific topic. A couple of leading doctors in the area have already contacted him to discuss the state of the art.

He is also interested in getting involved in veterinary medicine and currently has finished the first year of study towards becoming a DVM. His great love of animals is the reason he has put in hours of study on the creation of new species and the re-creation of some extinct species. He declares he is on the verge of re-creating Tyrannosaurus Rex.

He is also interested in athletics, but currently is slightly shy of his siblings in that field. His best achievement to date is to run a four-minute forty-five second mile. He declares that he is quite sure he can cut at least thirty seconds off that time, and he has made this a goal to achieve within two years. His second goal is to improve his time in the one hundred yard dash. He currently holds the school record of eleven seconds. He is certain that he can cut a full second off that time and possibly one and a quarter seconds. He claims that he can do this within two years as well.

As can be seen, all three grandchildren are highly ambitious and highly capable in the fields that interest them. My wife and I do everything we can to encourage them in anything they get interested in doing. The most interesting thing to my wife and me in all of this is that we never had any children.

THE WAITING ROOM

As he sat in the VA hospital waiting room to see his doctor, Jim Foster looked around and thought, "This place could use some brightening up. A plant or two would work wonders. I guess they worry more about allergies than about plants, as well as the problem of having someone take care of them."

Because he had grown up on a farm, he was partial to having plants around. Of course, his life had been altered greatly since that Improvised Explosive Device (IED) had claimed both of his legs below the knees. He was no longer a farmer. He worked behind a desk at a local insurance agent's office. Reasonably interesting work, reasonable pay, a reasonable life, but not the farming he had in his blood and had wanted to do for the rest of his life.

Just then the nurse called his name and he started forward in his wheelchair. He knew the routine here at the hospital quite well and was used to it. He had no other choice so he had learned to live with the process. He still had a lot of things he wanted to accomplish in life and not having legs had eventually become less of a problem.

One thing he would really like to change would be to not have to take all of the pain pills, which at times dulled his senses more than he liked. At those times, he was almost useless for anything or to anybody. That wasn't the way he used to be or the way he wanted to be. He planned to talk to his doctor about the possibility of reducing the number of pills he took. Could it be done? What effect would it have? What were the consequences?

As he rolled into the office, he noticed that his favorite nurse, Nurse Mills, was working today. She was here about every third time he came in. She was always ready with a humorous comment to lighten his mood and make him feel better.

Just as he started to talk to the nurse, the doctor entered and greeted him.

"How are things going today, Jim? Are you having any problems we can help you with?"

"No, Doc. Just the same old problems. I can't feel my feet and Nurse Mills won't go out with me."

Nurse Mills chimed in with, "You've never asked me out really. You just joke about it. If you ask nice, I might say yes. Try it sometime."

Jim hesitated, as the doctor sat there with a big grin on his face, while obviously enjoying the interplay. Then he asked, "Jim, tell me why you are here today. You really aren't due for another two months."

"I just fell in love with your waiting room and needed to come see it again. It's so warm and inviting. Yeah, that's it."

"Enough kidding around, Jim. Why are you here really?"

Jim answered, "I would like to reduce the number of pills I take. I think they are affecting my lifestyle more than my injuries. How much do you think I could reduce them by?"

"What I will suggest is that we experiment a little bit with that. Let's start with a 10% reduction for a month or two, then take another look. We will shoot for an overall 50% reduction. Do you think that's a reasonable goal?"

"Do I think that's reasonable? You're the doctor. What do you think?"

"We'll give it a try and see."

"That's what I like. A doctor with confidence," Jim said with a big smile.

"Why don't you talk to Nurse Mills while I write this up. She's better looking than I am anyway."

Jim added with a grin, "No argument there."

At that point Nurse Mills went out to the waiting room with Jim to finish some paperwork. When that was done, she went back to check some things with the doctor. During this discussion the doctor commented, "Did you know that he saved the lives of four of his buddies by trying to kick that IED away from them. They were only shook up but the device took Jim's lower legs. He was awarded a Medal of Honor for his actions that day. He well deserved it. I wish I could do more for him, but it isn't possible. All I can do is keep things under control. He has the strength and will to achieve great improvement when he really decides to do so. We will also start looking at prostheses as soon as I think he's ready."

Finally the nurse went back to the waiting room to get Jim's signature on several things and to set his next appointment. When that was done she said to him, "Since you are so bashful, I'm going to ask you to go to dinner with me. Pick your night and I'll pick the place."

"All right, how about next Thursday? There's a nice restaurant near my place. We could go there."

Nurse Mills responded, "I'll choose the place. I'll pick you up at 5:30 and I won't tell you where we're going. It will be a surprise. I have a van that will hold your wheelchair."

Thursday came around and Nurse Mills pulled into Jim's driveway exactly at 5:30. Jim was waiting by the front door. She helped him into the front passenger seat and loaded the wheelchair in the back of the van. She then proceeded to drive to a quiet little restaurant a few miles away. Going inside they were seated at a table near the back of the dining room. They talked until their food came but were fairly quiet while they ate. After the table was cleared they stayed and talked for two hours.

Twenty-five years later, as they sat in the airport lounge waiting for the plane to arrive, which would take their youngest child away to college, they finally agreed: Waiting rooms could be really nice places to visit once in a while.

WHERE WAS I?

I went to Brazil the other day. At least most of my e-mail buddies said I did. I don't remember it at all, but they all told me I had sent them the following e-mail:

Hope you get this on time. Sorry I didn't inform you about my trip to Brazil for a meeting. I am presently in Rio de Janeiro and am having some unforeseen difficulties here. It's so hard for me to believe this happened to me. I was robbed on my way to the hotel. All my cash and credit cards, as well as my cell-phone were stolen from me.

I need you to help me with a loan of $3,250 dollars to pay my hotel and meal bills as well as to get myself back home. I've been to the embassy and the police but they are not responding to the matter effectively. I will appreciate however much you can afford to send me. I will return the money to you as soon as I return. Let me know if you can be of any help. I don't have a phone where I can be reached right now so just reply to this e-mail and I will tell you how to send me the money. Please let me know as soon as you can.

-Phillip

The oddest part is I don't even remember flying down there. I must have really had something strong to drink or else I am starting to really show signs of old age. I don't even remember where I stayed or who I saw, so I can't verify that I was there, or what I did, or why I even went.

I asked my wife about it but she said she hadn't

missed me over the weekend. Of course she was tied up with getting ready for her book club meeting on Monday, her church ladies luncheon on Tuesday, and her church board meeting on Wednesday.

She carries quite a load with all that she is involved in, but you would think she would notice me sometime over the whole weekend. I need to quiz her some more on this while I try to figure out what happened. Maybe when I talk to her I will ask if it's a common thing that she pays no attention to me.

It couldn't be that I don't pay any attention to her. I compliment her on her hair all the time. I think. I'm sure I do. Almost certainly I do. I'll have to ask her when she gets home from wherever she is now. Whatever time that will be.

Now what was I going to check on? Oh, yes, I remember. The trip to Brazil! I remember going to Germany last year and to New Orleans four months ago. But Brazil? Good gosh, maybe I ought to see a doctor. What do they call the ones that check your brain? It will come to me later. I hope. I can always Google it. Well, I have some work to do on the computer as well as some e-mails to send out. I had better get them done.

I headed to the computer room, got comfortable, and turned the computer on, prepared to get busy for the morning. After staring at the blue screen for three minutes and wondering why it was taking so long to boot up, I tried shutting it down and booting up again. The shutdown procedure apparently was also not working.

What am I doing wrong on this? This thing has always worked in the past with no difficulty at all. Maybe if I just unplug it and let it rest for a couple of hours. Then it will do a self-search to try to determine what is wrong. Maybe that will solve the problem.

With that in mind I unplugged the computer and went out to the garage to try to finish some projects that I was trying to get done as Christmas presents for my three kids. In the garage I quickly busied myself with the projects and forgot for a couple of hours about the computer problem. Finally I remembered to get back to the computer, thinking to myself that it should be an easy problem to solve.

I plugged in the computer again and pressed the "on" button. The blue screen came up again but it didn't progress past that. No desktop, no folders, nothing. Over the next five minutes my playing with the keys produced absolutely nothing. As I got madder and madder I realized the computer was totally dead and unresponsive. What the devil is going on here? I have never had this happen before. I'm not sure what to do now.

I got out the phone book and started searching under the heading of Computer Repair. Then I spotted the ad for Computer Nerds. Their listing said, "All computer problems solved, viruses removed, upgrades performed, results guaranteed."

I immediately dialed them and, after a short discussion of my problem, made an appointment for them to come to my home the next day and see what was going on.

At 9:30 am sharp the next day there was a loud knocking on my front door. I hurried over to the door, opened it, and there stood a very nerdish looking young man. He introduced himself as John from Computer Nerds. He continued by asking if I had called about a computer problem. I said that I had and asked him to come on in. Finally I asked him why he hadn't just rung the doorbell. The response I got was, "I didn't see it." My first thought was, "It was right there beside the door and it's lighted," but I didn't say anything more. I just invited John to come in and then led him back to the computer room.

John quickly demonstrated his ability by plugging a portable pocket unit into the USB connection on the computer and using it to start up the computer. At the opening screen I jumped up and yelled, "It lives."

At that point I figured John probably thought, "And he considers me to be a nerd." With the opening screen of the boot up, John started some initial checks on the machine, exploring what was available. It quickly became obvious there was nothing available. It was totally cleaned out. No files of any kind, no folders, nothing.

John turned to me and said, "Everything on this computer has been wiped out."

At that point I sat down and put my head in my hands and moaned, "All that work gone. I didn't have the last six months of my work backed up. It is unrecoverable. I need to take computer classes so I can possibly avoid these kinds of problems. I should have done that years ago. I feel totally helpless right now."

John proceeded to completely check the computer out, looking for any viruses or worms. Finding none he asked for the backup unit and after installing Firefox as the new web browser he copied everything from the backup unit to the computer. He then did a complete new check for viruses and worms. At that point he told me that, at least for now, I had an operating computer and that was all he could do. He accepted his check for $100, packed up his stuff and headed out the door. As he exited he reached over and rang the doorbell twice with a smirk on his face.

I sat down at the computer and searched it for my backup list of contacts. I found there were only two hundred listed on it and I know there had been over three hundred before all this started. The next thing I did was to send out the following e-mail to what contacts I did have:

```
The last two days have been pure Hell.
Yesterday I received more than 50 phone
calls and no e-mails. A hacker had broken
into my computer and erased everything. They
deleted all 300 plus of my contacts. They
also erased all of my folders so I couldn't
let anybody know that my system was
compromised. They got past my security
settings and had all of my stored e-mails
forwarded to another address. The Computer
Nerds have fixed my security issues and I
have managed to restore a lot of my contact
list. Do not send me any money as the
previous e-mail requested.
```

I have now signed up for two computer classes, one on using and one on servicing. This way I feel I can get a much better understanding of them and hopefully manage my computer more intelligently than in the past. I'm already starting to feel much better about myself. The first thing I did was to change all of my passwords and made sure I didn't store them on the computer. I have also managed to regenerate my complete e-mail address list, as well as making sure that I back up all of my stuff every two weeks. Maybe for once I am doing something right with this computer.

THE CHEF

The head chef of the restaurant Creole Heaven had just finished preparing the Crawfish Etouffee for the expected evening crowd. His restaurant had been extremely busy with the annual 'Celebrate Our City Festival' scheduled for the upcoming weekend. This festival had become the high point of the year for their small town. It brought in over 50,000 visitors, and the revenues from it had become an important factor in the budget.

After everything was in the oven, he turned to check on the preparation of the salads when he heard a familiar sound. He turned, wiped his hands on his apron and went to the door to watch the horse drawn coach rolling down the middle of Main Street pulled by a team of eight Percherons.

"By gosh, there goes the Breaux family showing off again. They tend to act a little uppity rather than like regular folks just because they are the ones that started this festival twenty years ago." After he watched the coach disappear down the road he turned to go back into the restaurant to supervise his staff's final preparations for the crowd expected in approximately one hour. As he walked into the restaurant his maître-de called over to him, "You should go back to the kitchen. They need you to check something out. We just had a small fire in one of the fryers. It appears to only have damaged one fryer but we need to know for sure."

"Oh Lord," thought the Chef, "as sure as my name is Robert Boudreau I don't need this. Particularly on this day. I better get back there and see what's going on."

As the Chef headed back to the kitchen he glanced out the front window and noticed a car parked on the apron of the road with four people sitting in it. "They better move that car fairly quickly or they'll get a ticket," he thought. "Those tickets cost more during the Festival. They're almost certainly from out of town so I guess I should send someone over to let them know."

He hurried back to the kitchen and on the way asked one of the busboys to go out and tell the people in the car about the potential ticket if they parked there too long. In the kitchen he immediately got busy checking the fryer, making sure it was unplugged and reasonably cooled down. He decided he didn't have time to mess with it and could get by without it for the weekend. On that basis he told another busboy to take it to the backroom and leave it there for now. Then he finally got started with more food preparation for the evening. He was fixing three of his own favorite foods, Shrimp Remoulade, grilled cod in lemon butter sauce, and Shrimp Creole. All three usually sold quite well. Of course, there was always someone who wanted a cheeseburger so he was prepared for that as well.

He hoped to have everything lined up so his sous chef could manage things for about an hour and a half starting at about eight thirty pm. He had been asked to be a judge for the annual beauty contest. The man who headed up the contest said they had asked him to do it because they felt that, in terms of beauty, he was a true expert but they gave him no explanation of how they reached that conclusion. They were having a 'Mr. Hulk' contest as well as a beauty contest, but he was happy to only have to judge the beauty contest. His basic problem was he knew all eight of the young ladies who had entered. Their families ate at his restaurant regularly. He had tried to get out of being a judge but they had insisted, so he finally agreed to do it.

A few minutes before eight thirty the Chef arrived at the theater where they were holding the contests. He was escorted to his chair down front where he could see all the contestants easily. The other three judges were already in place. They included the Mayor, the Vice-Mayor, and the Chief of Police. At 8:30 pm sharp the music started up and the young ladies slowly paraded onto the stage, each one trying to put on her most elegant walk. Slowly they worked through the talent part of the contest as each of the girls demonstrated their capabilities in music and dance. One demonstrated her yoga talents and another, her athletic tumbling ability. They then went directly to the swimsuit part. The Chef was glad they had not allowed the girls' requests to wear bikinis since they all were under the age of twenty one, and some of those bikinis get rather small. The ball gown part was different since none of the girls wore a ball gown, just their normal, newest dresses, most of which had been bought specifically for the contest.

After the gown competition the judges gathered in a back room to discuss their notes and to try to reach a decision. Fifteen minutes later they came out and announced their final decision, making a point of the fact that none of the final rankings were unanimous. Finally the winner was announced and amidst the crying and cheering the Chef thought it was really touching when all eight of the girls came over to thank the judges. He thought it was a great way for the contest to end.

He got back to his restaurant about ten fifteen pm and saw that it was packed with diners, even at that hour. When he first walked in it appeared the place was so full that there was no room between the tables. He was quite happy to see business going so well that late in the evening. He immediately proceeded to help with clean up in preparation for a midnight closing.

Finally, after all the serving and final cleanup were done, the Chef headed home. His plans were to watch TV and read the morning newspaper and to try to relax until he dropped off to sleep, which he figured would not be long after the day he had had. He put his pajamas on, hopped into bed, turned on the TV and picked up the newspaper. In actuality all he got read was to finish the comics in the newspaper. At that point he was out for the night.

DECISIONS

It was in late summer that Mona lost her husband. It was a traffic accident and he died instantly when he went off the road during a rainy night. There had been four accidents along that stretch of road over a four-hour period. His was the only fatality.

Mona and her husband had not had any children, so this left her all alone and starting to wonder about her life.

On a day in the following November, Mona decided she no longer believed in God. As she left her house on that morning the dogwood tree beside her front door had blossomed. Mona failed to notice it for a while, but when she did she also noticed that the rose bush near the tree had also come into full bloom.

"That's odd," she thought. "What could have caused that in November?" Then she started to feel a warming in the air. "What is going on now? Why is this happening all of a sudden? I don't know of any warm weather fronts coming in. On the contrary, they are saying we should be having below normal very cool weather here for the next few days."

"Is God trying to tell me something? Do I need to rethink my life and my decisions? But since I have declared that I do not believe in God, why should I need to do that? What could cause all of this if not God? If that is true, then maybe I have made another wrong decision in my life. I declare that cannot be true. But how do I know for sure? I don't. I can't. Should I go fix supper or stay here and just give it all some more thought or maybe should I just pray? I need to talk to someone, but who? I can only think of one person that I could really discuss this with."

With that she picked up her cell phone and dialed the number of the local American Baptist Church. The phone rang four times before someone picked up and a calming voice said, "This is Pastor Johnson. I know you have questions. Let's discuss them."

THE FIND

As the Board meeting was winding down with everyone glad that it was finally ending, the head of the Technology Department announced that the new computers had just arrived.

He asked, "Does anyone have a good suggestion about what to do with the old, outdated computers after we download everyone's files from them. Our options are to recycle them, donate them, or just junk them. Suggestions anyone?"

Several people started speaking at the same time, and then, just as quickly, they all shut up and looked around. Finally, one of the Division Chiefs, Joseph Martel, spoke up and asked if they would be able to take any of the computers home, sort of a small bonus.

The technology director quickly spoke up, "That won't be allowed. The computers have to leave all connection with the company in order for us to get the tax break allowed by the IRS."

At that point several groans were heard around the room but no dissension. Martel said under his breath. "My two pre-teens could sure use a couple of those." Finally, the President of the company spoke out, "In line with the tax break our options are as initially laid out, donate, recycle, or discard. As I call out each option, vote by raising your hand. Vote only once or I will assign you to cleaning all the computer monitors in the company as well as spell checking all of the forms and instructions put together in the last week."

As everyone started to laugh, the President called out "Donate?" Immediately four hands went up. Then,

"Recycle?" Three hands were raised. Finally, "Discard?" At that point five hands were lifted.

"Well," said the President, "that makes it close but official. After all of the files are downloaded, the computers will be discarded. Anybody seen taking one home will be penalized on payday. Is all of this clear?"

There was a resounding, "Yes" and everyone started to rise and head for the exit.

"Wait a second. We have one more item to cover. Do we want to send the $200,000 to our office in Sweden to cover the extra costs of final development of the power station for our satellite communication system?"

After about ten minutes of discussion, everyone agreed that even though the need for the power station had diminished, the system would be useful for several other projects that were in development. Then they all quickly exited, heading back to their offices and hoping to be able to leave work fifteen to twenty minutes early.

The technology director stayed to talk to the President. He pointed out there were twenty computers to be replaced and he would get his people started on them first thing in the morning. They did not want to interrupt work more than was necessary, so they would pick up five computers at a time, and then each of the five people involved from his office would take one and work on it. This would leave fifteen computers operational at all times. The crew updating the computers would come in at night to do as much of the work as possible. It would be worth the overtime to keep things moving on everything else. Of course, there would be some finishing work each of the next days, but it was only expected to be a quarter of the day, maybe in some cases half of a day.

The company President nodded and said, "That sounds like an excellent plan. I fully approve of it."

With that they both got up and started back to their offices.

"I have to finish a quarterly report for the stock holders that is due in two days," said the President.

"Yes and I have to put together the list of computers and the order in which they will have files transferred to one of the new computers," the technical director responded.

The Tech Chief proceeded to finalize the plan and set everything to start in two days. His people were ready and anxious to get rolling on the updates. Actually, they were prepared to start sooner than later because of all of the overtime work that would be required.

Two days later the tech team collected in the office at 5 pm and waited for the first five computers to be delivered to the work room. An hour later with the computers sitting on the work benches things got rolling. The computers were hooked into the main frame and the work began. The approach was going to be, first, to download the files to the mainframe computer, then to prepare the hard drives on the new computers, check them out for proper functioning, and then to start the download from the old computer to the main frame, and then to the new computer. The files themselves were not going to be checked unless something created a problem. The process took quite a bit of time and had to be monitored constantly for glitches, which would then require starting over again with that computer. After four nights plus some extra time for finishing work on two of the computers the work was completed. At that point everyone breathed a sigh of relief and went back to their normal jobs and were glad to do so.

The procedure for dumping the old computers was initiated. It consisted mainly of stacking them on carts and finally rolling them out to the trash pickup area. There was no special rush as the trash pickup was not for three days yet. The two janitors proceeded to collect all twenty computers in one place and then to stack them on two handcarts. Actually rolling them out to the trash area would be done that evening as the regular cleaning was done.

At about 10:30 that evening, when the cleaning team got a little time, two of them grabbed the handcarts, rolled them out to the trash pickup spot, and then spent fifteen minutes carefully stacking them on the ground. There was some discussion of taking a couple of them home, but they finally decided doing that could and probably would get them in trouble with the company and might cost them their jobs.

When they were done they went back inside to start putting things away in preparation for going home. Thirty minutes later they went out the door, hopped in their cars, and drove away.

Two hours later, an older pickup truck came rambling along the road. Inside it George was trying not to lose his concentration on the road. Just because he had finished four beers was no reason for him to run into something. Or, at least, that was the thought that kept running through his head, and every few blocks he would state it aloud to his best friend, Marvin, sitting in the passenger's seat. Marvin very easily ignored him as he had had five beers. For him it was time for a nap.

As they rounded a curve George suddenly snapped

fully awake. There, near the road, lay a couple of stacks of some kind of electronics. As they drew nearer George could see they were computers, about fifteen or twenty of them. They had obviously been trashed and since George and Marvin earned quite a bit of money refurbishing computers, they were like a pile of gold laying there ready for the taking.

George pulled up next to the stack, hopped out of the truck, and started loading them in the back of the pickup. Marvin managed to sleep through the whole work of loading up and pulling away. He didn't wake up until they were in the garage at their place. At that point, after a few yawns and lot of mumbling of indecipherable words, he mostly woke up and slowly climbed out of the truck. He happened to turn towards the garage door and his eyes started to get very big.

"Wha-wha-what is all this? Where did these come from? Did you steal them somewhere? Tell me about them! Come on! Speak up!"

George proceeded to tell him the whole story, emphasizing that they were not stolen. They had been in the trash for the taking. He speculated that all of the memories had most certainly been erased so that anybody that got them would have to start from scratch and that all previous information on them would be gone. He then began to unload the computers and stack them against the garage wall. They would start checking them out in the morning to see if they could be refurbished and made useful.

The next morning George and Marvin went out to the garage and dove into the job of checking their new find, the stack of computers. They each took one over to their respective workbench, plugged everything in, connected a monitor, and started turning everything on. Almost simultaneously they both gasped loudly as the opening screen came up showing lists of folders and files. They never expected this. Apparently the company geeks had a glitch they had never checked for or found. When they cleaned up the files and erased the hard drive the action did not take. All of the original files were still there.

The two of them started looking at what was in the folders on these first two computers. They then started laughing at what they were finding. They proceeded to print out the listing of files. They then hooked up the next two and ran through the same procedure. This continued until all twenty computers had been checked. Finally they shut down the last two computers and sat down with the lists of files.

They found a lot of company data; most of it marked "Company Private" including plans for future products and much company financial data. There was also employee personal stuff such as emails to relatives and family pictures plus many notes to themselves about what they needed to get done after work. On two of them they ran across an extensive collection of pornographic files and pictures. They spent some time going through those. On two of the computers there were also some details of criminal dealing such as houses broken into, listings of stolen items, and even one computer that had details of one person sending restricted information to a competitor company. On one there was a file marked "Secret". George deleted it without looking beyond the "Secret" label. He did not want to get involved in anything like that. His father had worked on a classified government program, and he had always made it clear that a classified file was nothing to mess with. It would mean big problems, maybe even jail time, for an unauthorized person to fool with them.

They discussed, for two hours, what would be the best thing to do, and then they decided to delete most of the pornography, saving some of the really good pictures, and leave the personal stuff alone as well as the company related programs. Then they had a further long discussion of whether to notify the company about what had been left on the computers. In the end their final decision was to delete everything off the hard drives, including the pictures, and to go ahead as they had originally planned. In this way they could still eventually sell the computers, earning the extra money they needed and not destroy a bunch of people's lives. They decided that if the company geeks couldn't do their job properly it was not up to them to stir up a big mess.

In the end that was what they did, and the four thousand dollars they eventually got for the computers was a big boost to their college fund for the coming year.

HOW ABOUT A BEER?

"Aren't these Osher classes for seniors great?" Bob said to no one in particular.

"Yes, they are," replied two people at once.

The first lady, Mary, continued, "The variety of classes is excellent. I just love them. You can find almost every topic imaginable over the four sessions they have each year."

The second lady, Lottie, jumped in with, "I always take at least four classes and sometimes five or six in each six-week session. The problem is that it can be very difficult to get the classes you want."

"I see they even have a 'Dining in Dayton' class this session. I understand one of the restaurants is going to have beer samples for tasting during the third week," Bob responded. "This would not normally be allowed, but the restaurant owner had gotten permission ahead of time with the UD Vice President, Julie Masters, in charge of Osher."

"They always have fifty to sixty people in those 'Dining in Dayton' classes. The moderator would have to bring in, at least, three cases of beer. Maybe if we helped him bring them up to the classroom he would give us a bottle of it," said Lottie wishfully.

"I don't know if he is allowed to do that. It is probably against the law," Mary said.

Bob thought for a minute or so and then turned to the two ladies. "Just a thought. Maybe we could distract him and get a couple of bottles for each of us. All we would need is a distraction for thirty seconds to a minute. There must be something we could do. Ah ha! I have it. You're pretty hot for a sixty-five year old, Mary. Why don't you distract him and Lottie and I will grab a few bottles?"

Mary got a startled look on her face and said, "You sound like you want me to strip for him."

"No," Bob said, "just some flirtatious winking should do the job. Of course if you want to do a small strip tease it would probably be very effective. I would even try to get an extra beer for you."

Mary's response was, "I have a question for you, Bob. Where are you going to drink these and not be seen?"

That's easy. I saw an 'Out of Order' sign in the hallway. I would propose we put that on the women's restroom door and we could then have complete privacy."

"And what if someone saw you going in or out of the ladies restroom?" Lottie asked.

"Easy. I would just be the repair person fixing the problem," was Bob's answer. "Now we have a week to finalize plans. Let's get together at Doubleday's Restaurant and get this plan finalized."

That evening they met at Doubleday's, ordered a beer, and started discussing how best to accomplish their goal. After two beers and an hour of discussion they felt they had a workable plan. It was agreed that Mary would provide the distraction, while Lottie and Bob would do the deed. They had to make sure that Mary created enough of a distraction, and they all agreed that she should be able to accomplish that without any problem. They told her to make sure she wore a blouse on which she could undo the top button or two. Then she would have to ask the guy bringing the beer to step around the corner at the elevator to help her with her book bag which would be extra heavy that day. That should give them at least one to one and a half minutes. That would leave Bob and Lottie plenty of time to grab six bottles of beer and get the box closed properly so there was no sign of what had happened.

With that they finished their second beers, decided to meet at UD's River Campus on the first floor by the elevator in two weeks on Thursday at twelve.

"The class starts at 12:30 so the moderator will be getting there about a quarter after twelve. We will be there and ready for him," said Lottie.

Everybody felt their plan would work and they headed home to hit the sack or watch television.

Two weeks passed very quickly and finally it was Thursday. All three conspirators woke up early in expectation of the day. Among their plans was meeting in the cafeteria in UD's River Campus building. They would have an early lunch in preparation for action.

After eating they sat and reviewed their plans to make sure they hadn't overlooked anything. Finally, at a quarter to twelve, they arose and headed over to the elevator. Of course Bob had to help carry Mary's book bag, which he felt must have several bricks in it to make it that heavy. Mary and Bob went down the short hall beside the elevator, deposited the book bag on the floor, tipped it over, and then Bob went around to the elevator doors. There he joined Lottie and they stood there pretending to admire the view out the big window.

Finally, at 12:15 a man came down the hall from the front door pushing a handcart with a stack of three cases of beer. Bob could see from a distance that it was his favorite brand of beer. He thought to himself, "This looks like everything is turning out just right. Our luck is holding so far."

Just as the beer man got to the elevator Mary stepped around from the side hall, caught his eye, or one should say, her slightly open blouse caught his eye. As he stared she asked, "I need a nice, strong man around here in back. My class book bag fell off of the cart I was using to move it. I can't get it back on the cart. It is extra heavy because of some of the special stuff I was bringing to class."

Mary leaned forward a little more and asked, "Could you help me? I would consider it a very great favor." The tone of her voice got a little huskier and she could see him melting into a puddle.

"I, I, I think I could certainly give you a hand with the book bag."

As they headed down the hall Bob and Lottie prepared to make their move. Bob had brought an Osher red and black bag to put the beer into. They quickly and quietly ran up to the stack of beer boxes, sliced the top case open, pulled out six beers and resealed the box with masking tape they had brought along. Lottie picked up the top beer box, Bob picked up the second one and Lottie set the first one down on the stack. Bob then put the full box down on top of the stack. There was no obvious evidence that anything had been tampered with.

Bob and Lottie then quickly headed for the ladies restroom, put the 'Out of Order' sign on the door and went in.

At this point Lottie was in charge of the door and keeping people from coming in. In about five minutes Mary came to the door, gave the agreed upon knock, and entered the room. Then they each picked a stall, sat down, and opened their first beer. Mary, having a little fun, reached back and flushed the toilet.

Bob called out, "Hey, hey, hey, keep it clean over there. No matter how badly you had to go these are supposed to be out of order. What if someone heard that?"

"I was just having some fun. I won't do it again," was Mary's response.

"Now I have to go to the bathroom," Bob replied. "Just kidding. Just kidding."

All three sat quietly drinking their first beer. Several times they heard footsteps come up to the door and then proceed away, usually with mutterings of one kind or another.

Finally, after fifteen minutes of savoring some good brew Mary and Lottie decided they wanted to take their second bottle home and have it later in the day. They found they could tuck their second bottle in their purses, so they proceeded to do that. They dumped their empty bottles in the trash can and headed out and away with a final comment to Bob. "Remember, no flushing."

Bob started to work on his second beer, slowly downing it, and enjoying it thoroughly. Finally he prepared to clean everything up and get ready to leave. He tossed his two empties into the trash can and turned to the door. At that point there was a loud knock on the door.

"Don't come in. I'm almost through," Bob yelled out.

"What are you about through with in there, and why are you in the ladies restroom?"

Bob recognized the voice. It was Denise Qualtos, the point of contact for the Osher classes.

"One toilet was stopped up and I think I have it cleared now. I was a plumber before I retired." With that Bob flushed the toilet and walked out the door, took down the 'Out of Order' sign and said, "I'm all done here now." He then headed for the exit.

Denise stood there too astonished to speak. She could only stare at him as he headed out.

Finally, as Bob headed out the door she found her voice. "Wait a minute. I have a whole bunch of questions."

She was too late as Bob went out the door and was gone. He quickly made his way down to the parking lot and joined Mary and Lottie, who were still there discussing their classes. They couldn't stop giggling as they headed for their cars and home.

Half way through his class the 'Dining in Dayton' moderator realized some bottles of beer were missing. He checked around and finally decided he left them at the restaurant.

THE THIRTEEN MEETINGS

First Meeting

There it was again. That low noise.

It was coming from just beyond the bushes over by the lake. Joan was uncertain about what to do but finally felt that she had to go check on it, if for nothing else, just out of curiosity. She got up from the park bench and walked the thirty feet to the bushes where she could see the water on the other side. Then she saw what was causing the noise. There was a man lying there by the edge of the water. He was holding his leg and moaning in a low tone. As she came closer she could see the jagged rock laying there with what appeared to be a few drops of blood on it. The man was slowly rolling back and forth, moaning and sometimes cussing, all in a low tone. As she came up to him he rolled over and tried to move away from her. "Don't throw another rock at me," he gasped. "I'm hurt bad enough already."

"I did not throw the rock at you," she replied with a tone of indignation. "It was probably thrown by a passing car. Are you hurt badly? Should I call an ambulance?"

"It hurts like blue blazes," he responded. "What would you expect it to do?"

"Well, I can walk away and leave you there you know," she replied with anger in her voice.

"I apologize. Please can you help me up? I think I can make it back to my car with some help. Do you think you can support me?"

Suddenly she saw the blood all over his pants leg and quickly turned her head away. She then turned back, went over and helped him up slowly. She then helped him hobble back to his car.

"Thank you," he said. "I really needed the help. I think I can drive to the hospital. There is one fairly close to here." He hesitated a second and then asked, "Would you mind giving me your name and phone number in case I need a witness?"

She hesitated a second but then gave him the information he wanted.

Just as he started to get into his car he turned and said, "I really do appreciate the help you've given me. I apologize for anything I said."

Six months later they were married.

Second Meeting

There it was again. That low noise.

It was coming from the far side of the room. He looked over and saw a young lady sitting there by herself. She had a letter in her hand and was staring intently at it. It appeared to be distressing to her. He debated for a few seconds and then walked over towards her, not getting too near. On closer look she did not seem greatly distressed, just mildly so. He moved a little closer until she looked up and saw him.

"Excuse me, I am Pastor Raymond Jones. Is something wrong? Is there anything I can do to help?"

She seemed to shake her head yes but then immediately shook it no. "Nothing that you can do anything about." Intrigued, he walked over to her table to inquire further. She started to stand up, but then changed her mind and decided to stay seated. She laid the letter on the table and continued looking at him. Then, finally, she indicated for him to join her. He did so, very tentatively, not sure what was going on. She started to tell him the short story about what was happening.

"This letter is from my boyfriend of two years. He was here a little earlier and left this letter for me with the waitress, asking her to give it to me when I arrived. We came here quite often so he was aware she knew who I was. When I opened the letter I realized what it was all about. He was breaking up with me and couldn't do it face to face. The funny part of all this is that I had a letter in my purse to give him saying I was breaking up with him."

"Well," said Pastor Jones, "it seems to be mutual. Why did you seem to be bothered?"

"I wasn't really bothered. I was trying to suppress my laughter," she replied. "I guess it was a race to see who got their letter delivered first."

"Well, under the circumstances that is probably the best attitude to have about it. If you don't mind, may I join you for coffee and pie to celebrate? I'm buying."

Six months later they were married.

Third Meeting

There it was again. That low noise.

It was coming from the bushes to the left. Despite

Mary's trepidation her curiosity got the better of her, so she went over slowly to see what was making the noise and to see if anything was wrong. She tentatively peeked over the top of the two large bushes planted there. Then she gasped and her hand flew to her mouth. What she saw there were two people, partially unclothed. She stepped back and yelled, "Get a room, jerks!"

The female of the pair looked at her and opened her mouth to scream but instead jumped up and ran for another bush to hide herself. The guy just rolled over and lay there laughing. Finally, he said "How about seconds?"

The woman behind the bush called out, "Can you bring me my clothes, please?"

Mary picked up the clothes, trying to ignore the guy as he started to quickly put on his clothes, and carried them to the other woman despite her feeling that she should just get away from there as quickly as possible. As the other woman got dressed they started to talk about why she would do this out in the open. The answer given was that she was actually a lesbian and just wanted to find out what it was like.

As she finished dressing, the two continued talking about this and that. When the woman was finally fully dressed they walked towards the nearest restaurant to continue their discussion. As they dined they talked more about love and its problems. They found they were a lot alike and this led to their getting together later. It turned out they both were lesbians and they lived in New York.

Six months later they were married.

Fourth Meeting

There it was again. That low noise.

She looked over and saw the old man sitting in the chair, his head tilted down on his chest, snoring loudly.

"Can you keep it down please?" she called over to him. When there was no response she repeated it more loudly and finally got a response. The head raised up and slowly turned to look at her.

"It's bad enough in this place without you sitting there snoring like that."

He smiled a bit and responded, "I do what I do best. Besides, this place is not bad at all, even though they call it a rest home. So give it a rest."

"I've been here two years and you are the most impolite person I have met," she retorted.

"You mean you find me more impolite than the guy that sits here and breaks wind?" he asked.

"Well, maybe you have a point. There are some people here that are much worse. And you have been here longer than I have, I think. You said you've been here about four years. I've noticed that you are here by yourself. Were you married? May I ask what happened to your wife?" she asked.

"Cancer. I don't want to talk about it."

"My husband died of cancer also. Fifteen years ago, it was. Left me almost destitute. That's why I am in here."

"I am here of my own choosing," he said. "I got

tired of taking care of a house all by myself. Don't take this wrong, but would you like to join me in a cup of coffee?"

"Why, yes, I would, thank you."

Six months later they were married.

Fifth Meeting

There it was again. That low noise.

Harriett looked around and saw the little boy trying to sneak out the door. She quickly moved over, caught the door and pushed it shut.

"Where do you think you are going, young man?"

"I wanna go play," he responded.

"I think you need to go to the Principal's office. Now."

The teacher asked the student teacher to take over and collect the tests when the students were done. She then took the boy by the hand, led him out the door and headed down the hall with him in tow.

She heard footsteps behind her and looked to see who it was. Coming down the hall was the science teacher, Mr. Johnson, walking along holding the back of the shirt of a little boy.

He asked the lady teacher, "Are you headed for the Principal's office?"

"Yes, I am. I was left no other choice."

"Same here, Miss Blue."

"Amazing what these second graders are capable of doing. I just don't understand their minds sometimes. It is nothing like when we were that age," she said.

"That's so true," replied Mr. Johnson.

Twenty minutes later as they left the Principal's office, Mr. Johnson asked Miss Blue if he could buy her a cup of coffee in the cafeteria.

"Since it is now our break time and my student teacher will have collected all of the test papers, I will accept."

Six months later they were married.

Sixth Meeting

There it was again. That low noise.

It was the bus driver gently gunning the engine, ready to leave for McGinnis Center. As Harry got out of his car he thought, "Unless I hurry up I will miss this bus and it's fifteen minutes until the next one." When he got on he saw it was standing room only. "Darn, I should have gotten here ten minutes earlier or brought my cane. I get in a hurry and forget that thing all the time."

Just then a voice called out, "Hold the bus, I am hurrying as fast as I can." The driver waited patiently for the lady to climb the steps into the bus. Then she looked down the row and said, "Darn, I should have gotten here ten minutes earlier."

A man seated near the front got up and offered the lady his seat. She thanked him and sat down. Harry wound up standing in front of the lady, holding the overhead rail to try to maintain his balance as the bus headed over to the McGinnis building where class was held. She looked at him for a second. He nodded to her and said, "I'll try not to fall into your lap."

She then asked him, "What class are you in?"

"I have two classes this afternoon. The one on Dining in Dayton and one on Short Story Writing."

"I guess I will see you in the short story class then. I am really enjoying seeing if I have a creative side," she said.

"Yes. These "Learning in Retirement" classes are great for us seniors. Keeps our minds active while we learn lots of new stuff we never considered looking into before. And I really need it since my wife died three years ago."

"I am sorry to hear about your wife. My husband passed away five years ago. Heart attack. I still really miss him."

"Well, here we are at McGinnis. See you in class."

Six months later they were married.

Seventh Meeting

There it was again. That low noise.

It was just another car going by and not turning in. Bill stood there at the tennis courts looking around somewhat perturbed. "Where in the devil is that guy?" he said aloud, talking to himself. "He was due here twenty minutes ago. He didn't give me any indication that he would not be here today. I guess I'll hit a few more practice serves and give him ten minutes more."

As he walked over to the baseline and readied to hit a practice serve he noticed a young lady arriving in the parking lot.

"She looks very nice," he thought. "Oh looks like she is prepared to play tennis with someone. I hope she has better luck than I've had."

The young lady walked onto the courts looking to see which one would be most convenient. She looked over at him and asked, "Which court are you going to use?"

"Maybe none. My opponent apparently is not going to show up. Pick any court you like."

"Well I am just here to practice my serve. I don't have anyone coming," she said. "Maybe we can play a few games with each other just for the exercise."

"I would love to do that," he responded. "By the way, my name is Bill."

"I'm Josie. Let's play."

They wound up playing two sets and finding that they were very evenly matched. Each set went to 7-5, with each of them winning one.

As they drank some water and cooled down before going home he sort of jokingly asked, "Same time, same place, next week?"

"Yes, I would like to do that."

Six months later they were married.

Eighth Meeting

There it was again. That low noise.

It was his oxygen supply bubbling very lowly with almost a sound saying, "I am still here. I intend to stick around." He was 90 years old and had been in hospice for three weeks. When he was brought in he was not expected to last more than two days, but he was a tough old man. He hadn't made it to 90 by giving up on things.

The nurse came in, checked his vitals and the supply of oxygen in the tank. She then went over and looked down at him lying there in the bed. "I bet you have lived a most interesting and full life. I understand you were married for 65 years to the same woman," she said to him even though he couldn't hear her. "That's a record that not many people will best." She checked a few of the tubes going into his arms, re-arranged the covers a little bit and went to the next room. When she entered it she saw immediately that something had changed. The woman in the bed had moved the covers off her about two feet. She was supposed to be comatose. In fact, she had been totally so for a matter of two weeks. The nurse went over closer to check on what had changed. She noticed that the patient's eyes followed her as she approached.

"Mrs. Johnson, can you hear me?" The head nodded very slightly up and down then stayed still. A very slight smile appeared on her face. It was the type of smile that she had shown during her 88 years of life and the 62 years she had been married.

The nurse checked all of the gauges, verified that everything was all right and then headed out to talk to the staff doctor.

When notified the doctor came hurrying in and checked everything again and then leaned over saying softly, "Mrs. Johnson?" while watching for a reaction. Mrs. Johnson's head turned as her eyes followed him. That soft smile was still on her face. After thoroughly rechecking everything the doctor turned to the nurse and said, "I think we may be able to remove some of these tubes, a few at a time, and see what happens. She has made a miraculous recovery to this point. While I am here I will check on Mr. Burnett. I keep hoping for some kind of improvement in him."

As the nurse unhooked two of the many tubes in Mrs. Johnson the doctor headed next door. When he walked in he was bowled over by what he saw. Mr. Burnett raised his head off the pillow and looked like he was going to say something. This was amazing since he had not been able to speak a word in three weeks.

The doctor said to himself, "You would think that we were at Lourdes with all of the miracles going on here." He then paged the nurse and requested her to come to Mr. Burnett's room. The nurse was there in less than two minutes wondering if something had happened. When she entered the room she saw the doctor leaning over the bed checking Mr. Burnett's vital signs. The nurse started helping, all the time seeing Mr. Burnett watching them both, nodding, moving a bit when necessary, and still with that enigmatic smile on his face.

A week later all the tubes and hookups had been removed from both Mr. Burnett and Mrs. Johnson. The doctor decided they both could be moved out into the hall for short periods as a means of continuing their improvement and allow them to see more of what went on and to see all of the people moving up and down the hall. While in the hall, the two of them started exchanging brief comments and greetings and slowly progressed to longer conversations about their deceased spouses and their lives as they continued to improve.

Six months later they were married.

Ninth Meeting

There it was again. That low noise.

It was the cash register at the Golden Nugget, the best breakfast place in town, as person after person paid their check. The good part was that each time a person paid it meant that a table or booth had opened up for someone standing in the long line of people waiting to be seated. The basic problem was that since this place served the best breakfast in town everyone wanted to eat here. By 7:00 am they always had a long line of people willing to wait the thirty to forty-five minutes it took to get in and get seated.

John was thankful that he now stood at the front of the line. His stomach was saying, "Feed me." The problem sometimes was that since he was a single they seated people behind him at the bigger tables while waiting for one of the smaller tables to open. This didn't happen to parties of two or more. As John waited he thought about his deceased wife and his life with her. They had been married for forty years, happily, very happily. He missed her a great deal and thought of her often. She had been gone for only three years but it seemed like only yesterday.

As the receptionist approached him he was a little bit anxious. She asked him "How many in your party?" He could only say "one" and hope. She replied, "You may have to wait a few minutes. I only have tables for four right now. If you had someone else I could seat you at one of those right away." She looked back down the line and asked, "Are there any other singles here?" About twenty people back a well-dressed lady raised her hand. "Maybe you two could sit together. It would really facilitate things."

The lady answered, "No problem with me. I'm hungry." John indicated he had no problem with her joining him for breakfast. He knew he would probably eat and take off, never seeing her again. As the lady, her name was Harriett, came up to the front of the line John noticed that she was a very nice looking lady, maybe a few years younger than he was. A year or two maybe. He turned and followed her and the receptionist to a booth half way to the back of the restaurant. They were quickly seated and the waitress was there in less than one minute to take their orders.

John ordered the blueberry pancakes, stack of three, with decaf coffee. Harriett requested two eggs scrambled with sausage patties, hash browns and decaf coffee. Then they looked at each other, really for the first time. John introduced himself to Harriett and she responded with her name. As they started to converse, trying to find something to talk about, they also tentatively started to discover quite a bit about each other. Harriett finally talked some about her husband of 37 years who had passed away only two years before. They briefly discussed how their respective spouses had passed away. John's wife in a car accident, Harriett's husband of a fairly long debilitating illness.

They found that they both liked movies, plays, and

trips to Florida for sunshine and ocean swimming. As breakfast arrived at the table they almost didn't notice. The waitress had to slide their napkins over so she could set the plates down and refill their coffee cups. "How does it look?" she asked. Without a glance at her they both said together, "Fine, thank you."

As they ate they continued talking, getting more and more involved in the conversation. As they finished John said, "I come here every Tuesday and Friday before I go to volunteer at the Humane Society. Maybe you could join me on Friday at about 7:00 am. I would greatly enjoy not eating alone." Harriett responded, "Fridays I volunteer at the pet store on 8th Avenue. I have to be there at 9:00 am so breakfast here would work out quite well. Thank you for asking me."

As they walked out to the cashier John placed a hand lightly on her back to guide her some.

Six months later they were married.

Tenth Meeting

There it was again. That low noise.

It was the shuffling of Staff Sergeant Mary Hardesty's boots as she approached the line of soldiers. She was assigned as their sergeant during this orientation process. She noticed that there was only one female soldier in among the twenty-five in their semi-orderly lines standing at ease.

"It is always interesting to see their reaction to having a woman in charge of them," she thought. "Since they can't say anything adverse to a superior, their faces tell it all."

The line of soldiers were being prepared for deployment to Iraq on a special five-month tour to try to resolve some specific problems in one of the provinces. Their special training for this was just about completed and deployment was expected within two weeks.

"ATTEN-HUT!" Mary barked out as only a sergeant, male or female, could do. The line snapped to full attention immediately as they had been trained to do.

Mary walked up close to them trying to look each of them in the eye in turn in order to make sure they were paying full attention to her. She thought to herself, "I know they have been trained but they still look a little motley to me. I will work that out in the two weeks I have."

"Right face!" came the command and all did a right turn in place.

"Forward march!" came next as they all stepped out smartly. Mary noted that one of them seemed to do the commands a little better than the others.

"Maybe I can get him promoted to corporal to help lead this group on our mission. I think I am going to need all the help I can get to accomplish it."

Mary marched them to the education building in order to start their final briefing on where they were going and what they had to do. As they reached the building she called, "Halt," followed by, "At ease. Enter the building and go into the second room on the left." As they entered the room they noticed the windows were completely covered with sound proofing material, essentially sealing the room off from the outdoors. As they seated themselves a colonel entered the room and Mary called "Atten-hut." A few seconds later the colonel said, "At ease. Be seated, soldiers. We will now get into the full briefing on your mission."

As the colonel talked Mary watched her troops closely for anyone not paying full attention. She noted two that seemed to be doing some daydreaming. She also noted that her chosen one for corporal, his name was James Porter, was paying rapt attention and often nodding his head in agreement.

After one and a half hours the colonel asked if there were any questions, and after a half hour of answering the questions he indicated that the briefing was over. Mary called "Atten-hut" as the colonel turned to leave the room. Then Mary reminded the group that what they had heard was Top Secret and was not to be discussed or even mentioned outside of that room. She also informed them that they would be deployed in two weeks, that the mission would take about five months, and it was only moderately dangerous. She also said that it could be dangerous if they didn't stay aware, toe the line, and do their jobs right. With that she dismissed them to go back to their barracks to start getting ready to depart.

Two weeks later the twenty-five plus Mary boarded a C135 to travel to Iraq. The flight went smoothly and after landing they proceeded to their new quarters. The next day they got started on their new duties.

Five months later they were once again called to order and informed that they had performed admirably and would be leaving the next day for home. During the five months Mary had worked closely with her new corporal, James Porter. She had noted his skills in handling the men and achieving the goals of the mission. In working closely with him she had gotten to know him quite well and to admire his abilities.

On the flight home they talked extensively about their goals in life and their families, finding that they both were single and from large families with many siblings. Both were from the state of Ohio, although she was from Cincinnati and he from Cleveland.

After arrival back in the states they were then stationed at a small Army unit operating out of Wright Patterson Air Force Base until their respective discharges five months later. They continued to call and to talk to each other, managing to get together as often as they could.

Six months later they were married.

Eleventh Meeting

There it was again. That low noise.

John Thornton looked across the swimming pool noting the patter of bare feet on the concrete diving platform. He then watched the young man dive from the twelve-foot high platform. He noted the skill of the dive as the young man entered the water with almost no splash at all.

"Almost perfect," thought John. "I wish I could do a dive like that. Mine always look like I'm doing a biggest splash contest." As the guy surfaced from his dive John stood up, applauded, then walked over to give him a hand getting out of the pool.

"Great dive, fella," said John. "Where did you learn to do that?"

"I started to take lessons when I was four. I won a couple of regional contests held here in Vermont. I would have liked to try for the Olympics but I couldn't spare the time. By the way, my name is Bill Persall. What's yours?"

"I'm John, John Thornton. Do you think you could teach me to do something besides the cannonball?"

"Anybody can learn to dive reasonably well so long as they aren't afraid of the water."

"I'm not afraid of the water. I have been swimming since I was three," replied John. "I just never learned to do a decent dive off the high board."

Bill commented, "I will be here this coming Thursday at 3:00 pm. If you can be here I will start to show you the techniques needed for a good high dive. It will take more than one lesson, obviously, to accomplish the result you want. How about it?"

"Regardless of anything else, I will be here Thursday at 3 o'clock. Nothing will keep me away." With that he turned to leave, turned back to shake Bill's hand, and then hurried excitedly out the door to the shower/dressing room. Twenty minutes later as he left the building, he skipped a couple of times, jumped into the air and pumped his fist. "I am going to learn to dive properly after trying for twenty years to do it on my own."

Thursday arrived after what seemed like an eternity. John arrived at the pool eager to start his lessons. Bill arrived ten minutes later and found John all excited and worried that Bill wouldn't make it like he said he would.

"Just hang on. I'll change and be ready to go in less

than ten minutes." He made it in seven minutes and led John up the ladder to the diving platform. Once there he started to demonstrate the proper procedure to lead up to the edge of the platform, the number of steps he should take, and the position he should be in when he reached the edge. John ran through several practices on this part of the process. Finally Bill told him to go to the edge properly and to go ahead and dive so he could see what else was being done wrong. John complied, hitting the water with a splash big enough to seem like three people hitting the water at the same time. Bill started to laugh and then tried to hide it as John climbed the ladder again, but his shaking body gave him away.

"You better stop laughing or I'm going to shove you off the end of the platform."

"I will still make a smaller splash than you did."

"Then tell me what I did wrong," John asked, after also starting to laugh.

Bill gave him a fifteen-minute verbal lesson on the proper position for entering the water and what John had done wrong. John asked him many questions and tried practicing the position he was told to be in when he hit the water. Finally, Bill said, "Go again and try to do better."

John did another dive and Bill said, "It wasn't perfect but it was greatly improved." After ten more tries with some improvement each time they were ready to call it a day.

As they headed into the locker room they discussed the process of diving. Bill said, "I won't be here next Thursday. I have to make a trip home to see my parents."

John responded "That's OK. I can still come here and practice. I think I know what I need to do. It would be better if you were here to help me continue to improve."

"Maybe there is a way, John. My parents live only 300 miles from here and maybe you could go with me. We will have access to a pool that my parents belong to."

"I can do that. I have a few days of vacation coming and that seems like an excellent use of it. Are you sure that your parents won't object?"

"No problem. We have a third bedroom for guests to use and you'll like them. They are laid back and a lot of fun."

"OK, when do we leave?"

"In three days. We can go in my car."

Three days passed quickly and Bill picked John up at his house early in the morning. Three hundred miles sort of flew by as they talked about everything under the moon and the sun. They particularly enjoyed talking about their families, their jobs, and their goals in life. They also found out that each was a very accomplished musician, Bill on the piano and John on the clarinet. As they approached Bill's parent's house he pointed out that they were very liberal minded and that was one of the many reasons he really enjoyed his frequent visits with them.

After their arrival and all of the greetings and introductions, they were getting settled into their respective rooms when the call to supper came. As they were all getting seated Bill's mother said, "I am so glad

Bill has met a nice young man like you. He doesn't meet people easily."

Bill spoke up, "Mother. Later."

But she forged ahead, speaking to John, "You do know that he is homosexual, don't you?"

"No, I didn't know. But I have no problem with that since I am also."

Six months later they were married.

Twelfth Meeting

There it was again. That low noise.

It was the sound of the big sliding gate that separated the prison from the rest of the world. It was a minimum security prison, but it was still a prison and the gate still signified no easy contact with the outside world.

The total prison was divided into two areas separated by about one hundred yards. One was for male prisoners and the other one for females. All were in for less than a year on relatively minor crimes.

As the gate opened Walter stepped out cautiously. It had been six months since he went in, but that six months had changed his life. He understood what he had done and regretted it greatly. He had hurt himself and he had hurt his family, who had expected much better things out of him.

As he stood there holding the small duffle bag containing his belongings he looked around trying to regain the feeling of being free. Then he saw the van approaching that would take him back to the small town nearest the prison. Just then the main gate of the women's prison slid open. Walter looked over and saw a young lady step out and go through the same process he had. Just then the van drove up and stopped. He hopped in the back seat and leaned back to relax. His family was waiting for him in town for a big reunion and he was anxious to see them. Then the van pulled out and drove over to where the lady was standing.

"Oh great," thought Walter. "I have to share the van with her."

The young lady set her duffle bag on the front seat and climbed into the back seat, looked at Walter and thought, "Lord, I hope he doesn't want to talk."

After about ten minutes Walter asked, out of politeness, "How long were you in?"

"Five months," she responded. "I'm sure glad to be going home."

"That holds for both of us. I assume someone is meeting you."

"Yes. My parents are driving in from Ohio," she responded.

"Mine are already here waiting for me," Walter said. "Where in Ohio are you from?"

"Columbus. It's in the middle of the state."

"I know. I'm from Dayton myself. What's your name?"

"Margaret," she responded, not really wanting to know Walter's name.

They rode on in silence, enjoying the scenery and thinking of their respective families. Then they saw the sign "Town of Smithville." As they rolled into the small town, the van driver headed for the bus station, which was fairly close.

As they approached the bus station Walter saw his parent's car parked in front of the place. He was so anxious he was almost out of the van before it stopped rolling. He thanked the driver, grabbed his duffle and ran into the station, looking around for his parents. When he spotted them he hurried over and was exuberantly greeted.

"Before we head for home can I get a real meal in a real restaurant?" asked Walter.

"Certainly," his mother said. "I saw one just across the street. It looked decent."

As they headed out of the bus station Walter looked over and saw Margaret standing by the front window just staring out at the street with an unhappy expression on her face.

"What's the problem?" Walter asked her. "I thought you would be long gone by now."

"My parents haven't arrived yet. I hope they didn't get delayed anywhere."

Walter looked at his parents, then turned back to Margaret and asked, "Why don't you join us at the restaurant across the street and get something to eat? We can get a table near the front window so you can see your parents arrive."

Six months later they were married.

Thirteenth Meeting

There it was again. That low noise.

It was the male peacock shuffling around in the dirt trying to scare up a worm. When that didn't happen he turned towards the shed where he roosted at night and went inside.

"Rose, I think our peacock is in need of company and I don't think the chickens and ducks are filling the need," said Don as he headed over to the shed to check on the bird.

Inside the shed the male peacock was standing near the back corner just looking around, obviously seeking something. What it was Don didn't know for sure but he had a pretty good idea. He went back out to talk to Rose.

"I'm going into town tomorrow to the farm market. We need vegetables and I will be looking for something special."

Don was up early the next morning in order to get into town before the best vegetables were gone. It was one of the best attended farm markets in the state. On the drive he ran through his memory trying to recall some of the people who usually had unusual items for sale. Then it struck him. "John Foster, he's the one. I hope he's there and has what I want."

At the market Don went around getting the veggies and some other things they needed. He loaded these in the car and went looking for the Foster booth. Once he found the booth it didn't take long for him to purchase what he wanted and to load it in the back of the car. On the drive home he hummed and sang to himself, obviously very pleased by what he had done.

When he got home he carried all of the food stuff into the kitchen and then beckoned for Rose to follow him out to the car. There he showed her what else he had bought. She grinned great big and then started to laugh out loud.

Don carried their new acquisition out to the shed, opened the cage door, and let their new find out into the yard. There stepping out of the cage was one of the prettiest peahens Don and Rose had ever seen. She let out a typical peacock squawk and looked around at her new home. At the sound of the squawk the male came charging out of the shed to see who dared invade his territory. He stopped, looked, and you could see his whole demeanor change. He stood taller, he started to stamp his feet, and his huge tail opened up into a colorful fan. The peahen turned and walked away to explore her new area.

The male followed her stamping and shaking his tail feathers. The peahen finally turned around to face him and you could just see her grin.

Obviously, they were not married six months later, but they did produce many, many peachicks.

WHO WAS THAT MAN?

Two gentlemen were walking from the Victoria Theater to evening services at the First Baptist Church on Monument Avenue. They had been friends for a long time and their girlfriends had known each other since they were children. They all had remained close friends as they approached married life. They were also looking forward to many years of happiness and friendship. Since their girlfriends had a special girl's party (a bridal shower) to go to that afternoon, the two guys had decided to go to the theater together to see the play "The Devil and Daniel Webster." As they were strolling along they were enjoying the near perfect evening weather and the comradeship they had obviously shared for some time.

While they proceeded, they discussed good and evil in the world, whether there really was a Satan, and whether the church really impacted all of these things. They had had discussions about these things before with, in their minds, no certain conclusions.

As they approached Wilkinson Street, a man leaning against a lamppost caught their attention. He obviously radiated an aura that stood out. He was closely watching them as they approached. His smile looked normal until they noticed that the corners of his mouth turned down as he smiled; his eyes looked perfectly normal until they looked closely and saw the reddish glint sparkling in the edges of them; he was wearing a perfectly nice stylish Panama hat, but with a closer look they could see the two small peaks at each edge of the top of his hat; his face looked just like one of the neighbors until they saw that something about it enhanced the overall strangely evil look.

Just then the wind blew his hat off exposing the two sharp pointed horns. He then started to approach the two gentlemen. At that point the two, who were devout Baptists, ran like you-know-what for the First Baptist Church. Once safely inside they tried to relax and congratulated each other on their escape.

But did they escape? Only God and the Devil know for sure.

NOT MIGHTY YAR

The two sailboats were on a beat, heeled to almost 45 degrees in a fairly stiff breeze as each of the two skippers worked hard to get an advantage over the other. They were intent on the course and locked in on it, when suddenly Harry, the skipper of one of the boats, looked over at the other skipper and loudly yelled, "I'm leeward. Don't keep coming down on me. I have the right of way. If you don't stop it we are going before the race committee."

"What do you mean you have right of way?" George, the second skipper, retorted even more loudly. "You overtook me from astern and have to maintain your proper course. Stop coming up into me or we will take this to the race committee."

Then without a second thought Harry reached over and shoved George, not holding anything back. They started to argue right there, each bringing up some rule that he thought applied and that might give him some sort of advantage. All the while they pushed and shoved and tried to hit each other with their antenna. Giant insects? No, just two radio control sailboat racers with each one knowing with absolute certainty that he was in the right.

If this were big boat racing, the two would be yelling across the gunwales of their boats and would then continue down the course, but with radio control sailing they were standing on shore within arm's length of each other.

During the ensuing argument neither skipper paid sufficient attention to his boat and thus lost ground to the leader who had been only three lengths ahead of them. Due to their face-to-face argument and their obvious inattention to the racing, they were now about ten lengths back. While being so intent on each other they had lost sight of their positions and their subsequent losses to the leader. In fact they had actually dropped back to fourth and fifth place as two other boats got past them, while giving the two a wide berth to avoid any entanglement with their boats.

It went this way all around the course with more pushing, shoving and arguing and loss of position. Finally after all of the boats had crossed the finish line, they circled back to the dock, and pulled out of the water for the lunch break. At this point the two combatants started to discuss their lunch as if nothing had ever happened. They sat together talking, joking, laughing, and eating a sandwich. They had known each other and had been friends for over ten years. Their families often got together over the holidays and several times over the summer for outdoor barbecues. They had even taken trips together, sometimes for sailing, sometimes just for vacations.

Twenty minutes later the race director called, "Boats in the water. The start tape will begin in three minutes." The two skippers scrambled to comply and to then sail over to the area behind the starting line. They got there just as the two-minute countdown began. At the starting gong they hit the start line side by side in third and fourth place with both of them jockeying for position.

The two sailboats were on a beat, heeled to almost 45 degrees in a fairly stiff breeze as each of the two skippers worked hard to get an advantage over the other. They were intent on the course and locked in on it, when suddenly Harry, the skipper of one of the boats, looked over at the other skipper and loudly yelled. "I'm leeward. Don't keep coming down on me. I have the right of way. If you don't stop it we are going before the race committee."

"What do you mean you have right of way?" George, the second skipper, retorted even more loudly. "You overtook me from astern and have to maintain your proper course. Stop coming up into me or we will take this to the race committee."

OUR ORANGE TABBY

I've never told you about our cat. In fact, we have never told anybody about her. We didn't think they would believe us. Mostly she is a normal cat. She sleeps a lot, and she likes to have her meals at regular times. She can be the most lovable cat you have ever seen. She will buzz and purr and push for you to scratch her ears, her rump, her back, every part of her.

She is now eleven years old and really just coming into her own. For nine years of her life she was dominated by the two big male cats we also had. The two males have passed on and now her main goals are trying to take over and rule the house, along with helping us with everything we do. This includes deciding when we get up, when we eat, and when we go to bed. We have also found out that she is a great help at the computer. Spell checking is her best skill, but she also helps us when we balance our checkbooks on the computer. You wouldn't think an ordinary cat could handle addition and subtraction, but to our cat this seems to be a very easy process. The fact is she is better at numbers than my wife. I'm afraid to try any calculus on the computer for fear of what we might find out about her. The cat I mean.

An early indication of the cat's abilities was her reaction to a misspelling or a math error. She would proceed to growl loudly until the error was fixed. She would also growl when she heard someone say something wrong. The interesting part is she usually growls all the way through a political speech. She also seems to growl just to entertain herself. She even growls sometimes when we scratch her back, although she does seem to enjoy it. You can tell when she enjoys it if she growls at a lower volume. She also demands pay for all of these duties. She insists on special food afterwards. This includes Friskies with sirloin steak added in, plus some fresh whitefish as well. Obviously this can be expensive, but she strongly insists.

She works hardest at trying to rule the house. She decides when she wants to be fed, and this turns out to be four times a day, at the exact same four times each day. Sometimes she takes the notion to be fed in the middle of the night. She will hop up on the bed and head butt our hand or leg until she gets a response. Then when we roll over, look at the clock, and it says anywhere from three to five am we shush her away. Ten minutes later she is back again. The process starts all over again. The head butting and the shushing. Finally after two or three tries she seems to understand that it probably isn't going to work until morning, which in our house is after six am. That's when she tries her final effort, which is to bite because she is not being obeyed. If you are fast enough you may only get a small tooth scratch. If you are a little slow, plan on heading to the bathroom for salve and bandages. Again the point of all of this is that she just wants to make a point, because ten minutes later she is as nice as she can be.

I cannot explain all of this. I am starting to consider further consultation with an animal psychiatrist. But all he has come up with in the past is, "My gosh. I can't explain this. I need to study this cat a lot more to see what I can figure out."

If this were the only thing we had going we would have to go ahead with it. But actually we are also starting to try one other thing that may give us a chance to make full use of our cat's abilities, as well as to understand her better. We are training her to be an editor for a print-on-demand (POD) company. She has already been tested and passed with flying colors. This means she will start as an assistant editor. The people at the POD were amazed at the fact she did not make a single mistake. She spotted every single typo, word misuse, tense error, and grammatical error. She even spotted a couple of errors in French. The woman that controlled the testing was almost jumping up and down with joy when she realized how much help our cat was going to be for the company. They then offered to set up a pay schedule in which the cat's salary would increase by fifty per cent every two years after a modest salary for the first two years. I just wish my company would offer to do this for me.

The other thing the POD company liked is that the cat could easily put in a twelve hour day as long as she had a nap after lunch and she was fed her steak and whitefish additives in her cat food. And, of course, she had to have a scratching session every couple of hours.

The future is really starting to look great for our orange tabby.

www.ingramcontent.com/pod-product-compliance
Lightning Source LLC
Chambersburg PA
CBHW071345170626
46811CB00003B/994